TIME WITHOUT END

BOOK I

Ripples in Time

TOM TORTORICH

Green Ef🌳fect Media

Kansas City, MO
www.GreenEffectMedia.com

Green Effect Media

THE EARTH HAS ALL THE TIME IN THE WORLD.

—Oren Lyons

TO SEE A WORLD IN A GRAIN OF SAND
AND A HEAVEN IN A WILD FLOWER,
HOLD INFINITY IN THE PALM OF YOUR HAND
AND ETERNITY IN AN HOUR.

—William Blake
Auguries of Innocence

The Chronosverse

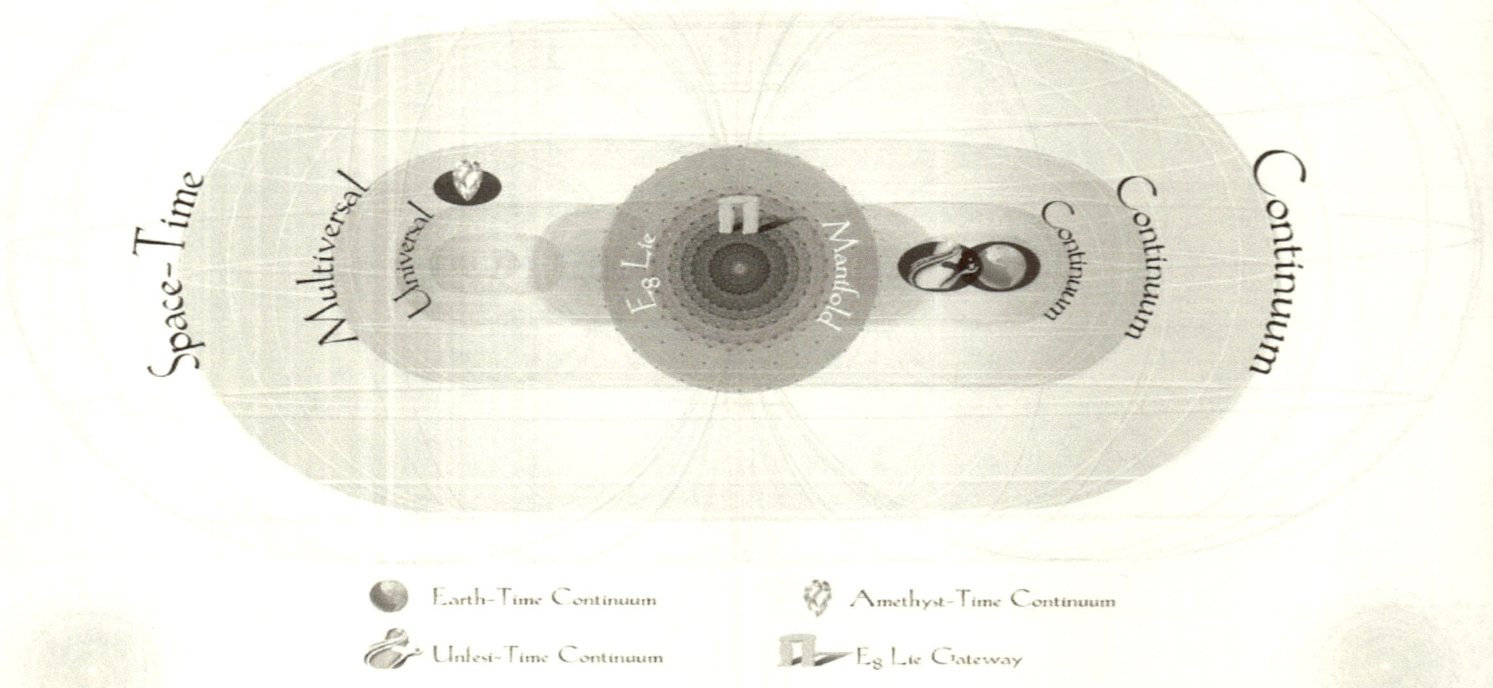

Continuum

Continuum

Continuum

Manifold

E_8 Lie

Multiversal

Universal

Space-Time

- Earth-Time Continuum
- Unlesi-Time Continuum
- Amethyst-Time Continuum
- E_8 Lie Gateway

E8 Lie Gateway

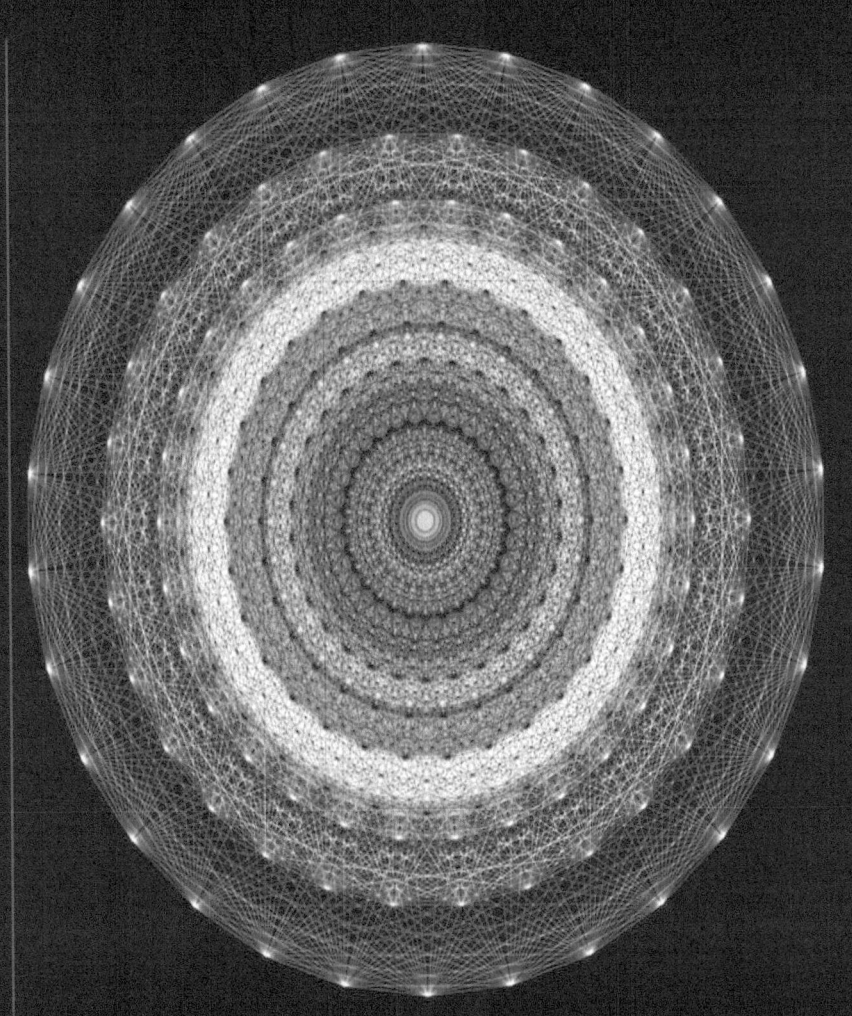

Contents

AUTHOR'S NOTE

I BELIEVE REALITY IS WHAT we make of it. I personally don't believe in the materialist world modern society has invented for the rest of us. We have lost touch with the natural world of Being and replaced it with a materialist, materialistic world. In my novels, my goal is to re-create the Reality we have lost.

In my non-fiction work, my goal to expose the underbelly of the "civilized" world, and raise awareness about global issues affecting us all.

In all of my creative work, you will find alternate realities created out of words, images, ideals and ideas.

You might think this is easier to do in fiction, but it's not so hard in non fiction as you might think. Perhaps that's because what passes for reality in our world is far removed from what I see it as--a world where all life is interconnected and One.

In my non-fiction works, I try to present readers with a different world view from the one our society teaches us from a very early age. I explore the notions that our obsessive quest for ever more, always better, always bigger, creates a world that works against our potential for happiness. What would happen of we place nature back in the center of life, instead of things?

That's easy for me to see and explain with "real world" examples.

In my works of fiction, I attempt to journey one step further, trying to envision peaceful, agrarian, harmonious societies who live with those ideals. That's quite a bit harder to do, because that means completely re-imagining a world that's utterly juxtaposed to the quotidian world around us--that means *the one (we think) we have to live in.*

THERE ARE A NUMBER OF scientific concepts, both modern and ancient, that play a key role in the adventure you are about to embark on. These range the full gamut from quantum mechanics to the theory that similarities exist between the ancient Mayan and Egyptian languages and cultures.

But don't panic!

A PhD, Master's Degree, or any other kind of degree (Farenhit, Celcius, or even the kind for measuring triangles) are neither required nor recommended to enjoy the ride.

I don't consider myself a scientist (because I'm not one), or even a writer (even if I might be). I'm just someone with an active imagination. In fact, about the only thing I can't imagine is actually, really *getting* things like Lie Algebra, the Schrodinger equation or the mathematics governing inflation.

I have read quite a few books popularizing string theory as well as the "Ancient Alien" hypothesis, and I'm hopelessly enthralled by any documentary narrated by Carl Sagan, Michio Kaku and don't forget Giorgio Tsoukalos with the crazy hair (he's my favorite).

For me, learning about their ideas has always been like lighting a spark in a room filled with imagination. Although parts of the story you hold in your hands are inspired and evolve out of real science, you don't need to fully grasp those concepts in order to *get it*. I tend to introduce a number of factually-based scientific concepts, explain them very loosely, and then allow all those loose ends to flail about in a torrent of imagination. Who knows what might happen next? That's the fun part. I like it when my imagination comes un-tethered from the laws of physics because that means the Universe of my stories comes un-tethered, too. So please, no letters telling me, "You so just don't get cosmic strings."

Nope. I really don't. But from what I think I do know about them, cosmic strings seem way cool. So why not have a little fun with them? Combine those strings with a trombone, throw in some sax, a piano or two, and a whole lot of imagination, and you wouldn't believe the cosmic harmony.

Remember, I'm just someone with an active imagination. And that's all you'll really need to *get it*.

I

EARTH-TIME CONTINUUM

C H A P T E R

1

RAISING THE HARD PLASTIC WINDOW SHADE would reveal a gateway into another world. At least that's what Erik imagined as a boy. But this was no childhood fantasy. He hesitated for a moment with his thumb and forefinger poised on the flat handle of the drawn shade. This actually would be a window into another world, offering a not-so-parallel view of reality to the one he had just witnessed in the third-world.

From his window seat in first class aboard the757, Erik Nichim pushed up on the shade and revealed an orange blanket spreading like wildfire across the night sky, creating the illusion that the world below was burning. The glowing embers of light pollution lapping up the sky over Chicago was the first unmistakable sign that Erik had finally returned home.

Beginning their descent just outside the city limits, Erik could decipher thousands of individual points of light on the ground, street lamps, automobiles and buildings, all arranged in a symmetrical grid, each one casting a ray of light into the sky and together projecting a translucent wall that fortified the metropolis.

The night had held dominion for much of the flight across the Atlantic, but now on the horizon, hazy behind the veil of the urban jungle, the first embers of dawn—a band of crimson crowned in cerulean blue—arched over Earth's curvature.

There's something wrong with this picture, Erik thought. Out of all life on Earth, why were humans the only species to look at the world with the desire to drastically change it—an obsessive compulsion to replace thousand-year old jungles with skyscrapers? The Chicagoland area was paved, landscaped, developed or in other ways a scar upon the surface of the Earth for a hundred miles in any direction.

What if our earliest ancestors could see the world as it was today? They'd never suspect it was theirs, or that we were them. Would they fear us, or worship these beings who could fly over the world, observers from the sky, from heaven, the once-sacred vantage of the gods? Perhaps our ancestors, witnessing the world we created, would simply look up at night and wonder, what on Earth happened to all the stars?

Flying from Madagascar to Chicago, Erik was astonished by the vast network of cities sprawling across the continents, glowing in an endless network of gangly, artificial limbs.

Erik had travelled nearly ten-thousand miles in the thirty-six grueling hours since his taxi had peeled out of the station in Ambalavoa. Mobs of Malagasy people had swarmed the streets for a mile along the thoroughfare leading to the American Consulate. Erik remembered how his taxi had parted the sea of people at an agonizingly slow two kilometers-per-hour. Walking would have been quicker, but the car was a bullwark against the angry mob. Protesters pounded their fists on the hood of the station wagon when they looked in to see its passenger was a *vazaha*.

The iron gates of the consulate promised Erik a warm welcome if only he could make it through this final gauntlet. All told, there had been fifty-eight American aid workers spread haphazardly throughout the country when the riots began. Now they all were being evacuated. American military helicopters waited to air lift the volunteers from the island. At first Erik thought the men in fatigues at the Consulate were Malagasy troops. He'd no idea the U.S. had a military presence in Madagascar. Being hustled into a chopper in small groups by men with machine guns was unnerving to say the least.

From the chopper to a pair of single engine planes, Erik felt like a stone skipping across a hopelessly large pond as his group made its way up the east coast of Africa.

It was eighteen hours later the next time he saw a clock, when their military escort delivered them to a commercial airport in Cairo, handing each of them a first class ticket back to the States.

In the mad dash to leave, there hadn't been any time for Erik to contact his family back home to tell them they were being evacuated. He thought about sending an e-mail from the airport in Cairo, but a quick look at the time-stamp on the ticket quickly quashed that idea. It would just have to wait.

The small group of evacuees Erik travelled with had talked about nothing other than the lives they were leaving behind in Madagascar.

They all seemed to share the same sentiment. It was such a shame they had to leave in the middle of the crisis. The political coup-de-etat had thrown the country into chaos, and the Malagasy people needed them now more than ever.

Erik was on a completely different page. For one thing, weren't they even the least bit concerned for their own safety if they stayed in Madagascar? One evacuee might later go on to volunteer in fifty-eight other countries. Fifty-eight dead aid workers in Madagascar would help no one.

Dear (name here),
We regret to inform you that (name here) was killed in Mada-gascar because he/she was incredibly naïve.

The only thing worse than a naïve volunteer is a naïve volunteer you have to listen whine for eighteen hours. Erik was relieved to find out they all weren't boarding the same flight in Cairo. Under the pretense of missing his plane, he left the others at the terminal where they continued sobbing, embracing and exchanging e-mail addresses and promises that they'd stay in touch. For his part, Erik couldn't wait to put this chapter of his life permanently behind him.

He remembered hearing that the worst kind of culture shock kicked in after returning home. Some people who spent significant time abroad found it hard to re-adjust. Erik never thought that would be him, not in a million years.

As THE 757 MADE ITS descent into Chicago, and Erik could see the little cars crawling like ants on concrete passages between a hundred thousand houses that looked like Monopoly pieces from above, he felt intensely claustrophobic, anxious and overwhelmed.

Debarking the aircraft only made things worse. O'Hare was a bustling zoo of people frantically scurrying about, many talking or e-mailing from cell phones while taking long, quick strides on moving walkways and casting irritated glances to anyone who dared stand still.

There was a mob at baggage claim whose size and temperament seemed to rivaled the political protesters in Madagascar.

Erik wasn't in a hurry because he didn't really know where he was going. His parents still didn't know he was back in town, and since he'd planned to spend two years abroad, keeping a house key was the furthest thing from his mind. The odds of them being home were slim. They were probably off on another one of their speaking tours somewhere.

Erik considered his options.

All his contacts were stored in his cell phone. No service in Madagascar, so no cell phone, so no phone numbers. He parents' home number was the only one he knew by heart. What an antiquated notion. Who needed to waste the time and effort to memorize phone numbers anymore?

Erik had been born just before the digital revolution. Standing there now, no phone, no laptop, no mobile internet, no American currency, Erik felt like a puppet who realized his strings had been cut.

A thousand little things people rarely thought about tethered them to their lives—things that just weren't a part of life in Madagascar. It was astonishing to truly comprehend how dependent civilization had become on technology. And the addiction was growing stronger with every passing day.

Was this one of the reasons culture shock hit hardest at home? Erik would be forced to re-consider if this really was his home. It certainly wasn't the same world he had been born into. Living in Madagascar really drove that lesson home.

Erik fumbled around in his pockets. He had a passport, an Illinois drivers's license, a couple hundred Malagasy francs—not worth the ink they were printed with on this side of the world—and a credit card.

Think, Erik.

If worse came to worst, he could get a hotel of course. But he wanted to check on his parents' schedule, to see when they might be home, or at least shoot them an e-mail telling them that he was back.

Erik spotted a gray-haired man in a business suit on an iPad. Erik had never used one. In the isle of seats across from the man, someone else was on a laptop.

The man looked at him suspiciously when he approached.

Erik was generally clean-cut, but now he wore two days of stubble on his face, clothes that carried the red mud stains of Madagascar, and unruly hair. The man's suspicious gaze turned to a look of apprehension when Erik asked if he could use the man's computer.

"Please, I just got off a plane from Africa, and I really need to get in touch with my parents," Erik explained.

The man's expression suddenly softened. "You look like hell," he said, with sad eyes. "Here, sit down."

"Thank you," Erik said, a bit bewildered when the man simply handed the computer to him.

"My daughter's going to Africa in a few months," he confided. "Volunteering at a hospital in Kenya. I hate the idea."

"My parents did too," Erik said.

He didn't much feel like making small talk, and used the lull in the conversation to log into his e-mail account and found the link to his parents' online calendar. Maybe no one memorized phone numbers anymore, Erik thought, but user names and passwords? Everyone probably knew a dozen without thinking about it.

He found what he was looking for, and it was good news. His parents were on one of their publicity tours, but tonight they were speaking here in Chicago, at a convention center not far from the airport.

Erik handed the laptop back to the man. "Thanks again."

The man nodded and handed Erik a business card. "In case you have any advice for my daughter. E-mail me and I'll pass it along. I'm sure she'd like to talk to someone who's actually been over there."

"Just tell her it's nothing like she expects—not even coming home."

SIX LANES OF TRAFFIC WHIZZED in each direction of the tollway. The sheer speed of the cars was dizzying. Never would Erik have thought he could forget how frantic life was in a big city, but this felt like he was experiencing it for the first time.

"How was your trip, my man?" the taxi driver asked in a thick accent as they wove through traffic, swerving from one lane to another.

"Well it was no vacation," Erik said matter-of-factly.

"Oh, I seeee. You didn't spend all your money, I hope, eh? Heh-heh. I hope not."

Erik knew where this was going. No different than Madagascar. Everyone wanted something.

"No."

"Oh, that is very good my friend, so you pay with cosh, yes?"

"The sign says you accept credit card."

"Yes, my friend, but I need the cosh so I can buy the goss."

Gass. Erik heard that one before.

Most people probably recognized they were being scammed, but didn't know exactly what the con was, making them the ideal prey. Credit card fraud was all over the news, which was naturally people's first thought. So they played it safe and used cash so the driver didn't get their card number. But this was about avoiding credit cards. Cabbies wanted their fare in cash to avoid the fees, and in some cases, get away with not reporting the money at all. It was fairly harmless, but illegal nonetheless. It played on people's fear more than anything else. If the driver simply told the truth, it would have evoked compassion, and the gambit wouldn't have offended Erik at all.

"This is it, here," Erik said.

The driver pulled into the horseshoe driveway where Erik noticed a large crowd. Maybe his parents' lecture had just ended.

"Nine-sixteen, my friend," the driver said, looking at the meter that read $9.60.

For nine dollars and sixty cents, Erik was surprised the driver even tried it.

Then again, the con itself wasn't exactly a Ponzi scheme.

"You prefer cash?"

"Yes, my friend."

Opening the door, and leaning halfway out of the cab, Erik reached into the front seat with a few rolled-up bills between his thumb and forefinger.

As soon as the driver reached back to take them, Erik

pointed with his other hand, "I think the closest gas station is just up the road, there."

Erik hopped out of the cab, with two quick pats on the driver's back. "But you probably already knew that," he said.

In the dark, it would be several long seconds before the driver realized the bills were Malagasy currency. By then, Erik was lost in the crowd.

ERIK DIDN'T REALIZE HOW MANY layers of grime and dirt were matted to his skin until he splashed cold water on his face in a bathroom more luxurious than Madagascar's presidential palace. He rinsed his glasses clean and dried off with a handful of paper towels. Better. A change of clothes and a shower would help, too.

A little more refreshed, Erik made his way back towards the hotel lobby, looking for signs pointing to his parent's convention area.

At first he thought he was in the wrong place. The posters on the walls and pamphlets piled atop various tabletops looked like they belonged more at a science fiction convention than a lecture on linguistic anthropology.

Erik's parents were both professors and, six months ago, had finally published the book they had been working on for the past decade. Erik had read bits and pieces of it—interesting, but most of it very dry.

It was released when Erik lived in Madagascar, and this was the first he was seeing of the marketing incarnation of their work. His mother was right. She described in her letters how the publisher was billing it more like a Hollywood movie than work by credible academics.

Erik found the lecture room, though their presentation was clearly already over. A small number of people lingered with empty plastic wine glasses in their hands, some thumbing through copies of his parents' book that were stacked to form waist-high pyramids on the floor along the walls. As if the pyramid stacks weren't tacky enough, the book's dust jacket depicted half of the Great Pyramid of Giza, blended down the middle into the non-as-famous Mayan Pyramid at Chichen Itza.

A compelling enough cover, it probably was a huge disappointment, if not an embarrassment, for his parents. Their hopes for the book were for it to invite comparison with Noam Chomsky, but the artwork seemed more appropriate for the latest television incarnation of Stargate.

Erik surveyed the few remaining faces in the crowd, wondering if he'd recognized anyone. A man with a distinguished salt-and-pepper hair with his back to Erik looked vaguely familiar. Erik didn't have time to wonder where he knew the man from.

"Erik!"

He turned around, right into a great bear-hug from his father.

"What ... what happened to Madagascar?" the bushy-bearded man asked.

Erik gave a lopsided grin, "Nothing. It's still there."

"I mean, why aren't you still there."

"All the volunteers were recalled," Erik said nonchalantly.

"Oh my God! Erik?" his mother cried. "You look so skinny.

What have you been eating over there? Rice and beans?

"Kind of. I don't eat beans," Erik said.

"What happened?"

"It's a long story. How's the book tour?"

His parents looked at each other.

"That good, huh?"

"You must be starved. Let's get you something to eat."

"I'm more exhausted than anything. Let's just go home."

"But all we have at home are frozen pot-pies!"

"As long as it's not rice."

C H A P T E R

2

SOMEWHERE ON THE UPPER IOWA RIVER

I
T HAD TAKEN A DAY AND a half, a helicopter, a pair of single engine planes, and two commercial jets to return to civilization. It was only a five-hour drive to get away again.

Erik was never much for city life, and after spending two short days at his parents' house in Chicago, he remembered what Pierre, one of his only Malagasy friends, told him to do just before he left.

"You take your little raft out on that water you tell me about back home and you forget about all of this, you hear me? You

lucky son of a bitch! Get out of this country."

It had barely registered when he'd said it. Erik's mind was elsewhere. Now that he thought about it, he realized it was good advice. Erik needed to go somewhere peaceful and serene to collect his thoughts.

His life had just thrown him a huge curveball, and he really had no plans at all for what he was going to do now.

"I need to go somewhere to think," Erik told his mom. "I can't do that with all this hustle and bustle around me."

"Well," she said, looking him in the eyes with a mix of joy and sadness. "It's my same little Erik who left a year ago trying to save the world. You're still restless."

"I'm not the same at all," he said indignantly. "I don't want to save the world anymore."

She smiled, "I'm just glad you're back in this country. After letting you go to Madagscar, I suppose I can deal with you going to Iowa for the weekend."

IT WASN'T A RAFT HE'D told Pierre about, but a canoe. And as far as Erik was concerned, the only place to go canoeing was the Upper Iowa River.

So here he was.

Sweeping through the river with slow, steady pulls on the current, the water dripping off his paddle transformed into liquid twilight as the canoe drifted lazily downstream.

Life out here made sense to Erik—one of the few places it did. On the river, everything else drowned in the movement of the water and the soft summer breeze. It was as though the ribbon of water didn't flow into the rest of the world. The calmness of just floating along, simply being, filled Erik with a sense of euphoria he found nowhere else. It was the meaning of life. And the rest of the world was only vaguely aware of it.

The sun was setting behind maple-shrouded limestone bluffs rising on either side of the winding river. Although the days were getting longer and twilight lingering later, it would be dark soon and Erik thought they'd better start looking for a place to camp.

Sitting at the front of the canoe, Erik looked over his shoulder at John, the friend from college who'd introduced him to the Upper Iowa River.

"So when you said we were going to camp on the river, what did you mean, exactly?" Erik asked.

John shrugged. "I meant on the river. Relax. Drink your beer."

By himself, Erik would have needed a specific plan, but John took comfort in not having one—especially out here on his river. His friend was right: Erik needed to relax. That was the whole point of this trip.

For the first time in almost longer than he could re-member, Erik's jittery nerves were finally beginning to calm themselves. The beer was definitely helping.

"Look," John said. "It's perfect." He indicated a distant point down river that Erik couldn't quite make out.

"Perfect for what?" he asked.

"To set up camp. What else? I mean, no one can know anymore when there's gonna be a flash flood, but aside from that."

"A flash flood? Are you shittin' me?"

"No shit, man. The water can rise prol'y fifty feet in a few minutes."

"You can't be serious. You're not actually worried about a flash flood, are you?"

"It's been dry enough yet, so we should be all good," John said, offhandedly. Then, as an afterthought, "Pro'ly."

"Are you just making this shit up?"

"Happened once. I'd never been so scared in my life. The first thing you do is stop, man. S-t-o-p. That means, stop, think, orient and plan, man."

He'd probably read that in some nature survivor guide. "Uh-huh. Then what?" Erik asked.

"Then you just look at the river. Then you look at the shore. Because you have to know where you are. I mean, exactly where you are. When I did that, when I s-t-o-p .... e-d ... I remembered there was this really old tree. One of the oldest, tallest ones in the county, maybe the whole state. Hell, this side of the Miss'ss'ppy, pro'ly. The water swept me away right to the tree and I grabbed onto a limb for dear life. Man I was stuck there for hours! The water rushed at my legs. My knuckles felt like they just couldn't hold on for another second. Fuck!"

John's breathy whisper of the profanity drew out the vowel for an unreasonably long time.

Erik's laugh came out as a single, thunderous belly-roar, "Hrhah!," and he decided another beer would do him good, so he reached into the cooler.

"Did I say something funny?" John asked.

"You're full of shit."

"No way, man! I mean ...wait ....Why? You haven't been in a flash flood, have you?"

"Just the rainy season in Madagascar."

"That's right! You went to Madagascar. I still can't believe that! Fuck!"

It had been a while since John had seen his friend. How could he have forgotten this was the one person who didn't let him run away with his stories. No matter how wild a yarn it was, Erik had first-hand knowledge about almost anything. *The fucker knows everything! Fuck!* John thought.

"So I take it you act'lly been'n a flash flood?"

"More like a monsoon. The streets in the village I lived in weren't paved, and they literally became rivers of mud."

"Well, hell, monsoons," John said, cashing in on his chance to salvage some dignity. "I mean a monsoon is one thing, sure, but flash floods, man. Fuck! Whole different beast. Let me tell you right now, if you're ever in a flash flood, find a tree. That's the key to survival. The only way you're going to live to tell the tale. A really old tree. Not so old that it's rotted through, though. But old. And really tall. And when you find it, you gotta just hold on for dear life."

Good story, check. Sound logic, check. What could Erik possibly say about *that?*

"I bet that strategy wouldn't work if witches sent the flood."

"*Witches?* Fuck! No, man, I bet that shit wooden work then. Hell no. Not if there were witches. But I don't know. I mean, I think you're safe. Where the hell are there gunna be witches?"

"In Madagascar. That's what they said, anyway. The people stay inside as much as they can during the monsoon season. They're very superstitious. They believe the rain is sent by a *pamosavy*. Everything in the villages is practically closed for two months straight—the market, the school, shops, everything. Because, you know," Erik said in a condescending tone, "not only do the *pamosavy* send the floods, they can kill you with lightning, or make you one of their sex slaves."

"That is fucked up!" John said. "Sex slaves.... like the witches are into bondage and shit?" He was trying to be funny, but John felt a heavy silence.

"What did I say?"

Erik's memories took on a life of their own. He had to say something, anything to keep their spell from sucking him in any deeper.

"Her name was Ellia," Erik said. "But I'm not drunk enough yet to tell you that story."

John laughed and returned his attention to the river. The sun was precipitously close to the horizon, but the good news was they were almost at the place he'd pointed out earlier. And it was looking like an even more promising campsite than he'd thought.

The river was only a few hundred yards wide and both shores were overrun with vegetation, hopeless for building a tent or a campfire. But smack dab in the middle of the river sat a flat island of gravel interspersed with shrub-brush jutting its head a few feet above the water.

Erik noticed that John was heading right for it. "You want to camp on a sand barge?"

"What the fuck."

"Have you camped like that before?"

"Nope," John said with confidence.

Well, do wonders never cease? John picked now of all times not to let his bravado get the best of him. "Would it have killed you to say, '*Sure, man, a bunch of times?*'" Erik asked. He would have felt better about all this if John told him he had.

"Well, come to think of it—" John said.

"Give it a rest, man."

He shrugged, "I tried."

John backpaddled against the current and ran their canoe aground on the gravely shore as a blue blanket of translucent light descended over the watery world. The two men quickly set up their tents, then waded to the nearest bank to gather firewood.

Soon their campfire was hard at work defending them against the darkness and providing heat for warming dinner. John cracked opened another beer—this time a long neck bottle of something fancy and German.

"Here's to you, Erik, and your triumphant return to the Western world," he said.

"More like returning with my tail between my legs, but thanks anyway."

"Well, I'm glad you're back. Gives me someone to canoe with anyway."

"Which gives me a chance to get away from it all."

They'd been making this trip throughout college, canoeing a remote stretch of the Upper Iowa River just outside Decorah, a small city tucked between limestone bluffs on a landscape that was folded like a rumpled blanket.

The unique region of Northeast Iowa possessed few of the characteristics that thinking about Iowa typically brought to mind. Iowa was synonymous with corn fields, soybean fields, Field of Dreams, and any other imagery that involved, in one way or another, flat, drab fields. Not bluffs, hills, pine forests or the Upper Iowa river that flowed majestically through all of that. The landscape had really surprised Erik the first time he'd come up here—almost as much as how John had every bend of the river committed to memory, knew the distance between every bridge and the height of every bluff.

John explained that the area around Decorah had been as far south as the glaciers had come during the last ice age. When the ice retreated, it left behind the breathtaking countryside. At least that's what happened in John's account of Earth's geological history. It sounded plausible.

Either way, it was beautiful, and these canoe trips were always something special for Erik. Some of their trips were rip-roarin' drunk ones, more drinking and playing *tippy-canoe* than anything else. John's father demonstrated the best way to win by drinking a beer while standing on his head in the center of the canoe. His father was a professor of mechanical engineering at the local community college, and remained absolutely convinced that as long as he kept the center of gravity low, the canoe would never tip, right until it did.

In stark contrast, other runs were the sobering ones that Erik came away from feeling completely at peace, in touch with the harmony of the universe. Some of the best times of his life were on those trips. There was an otherworldly sense of peace about being here.

They would canoe for hours without seeing anyone.

Where they camped tonight was one of the most remote stretches on the whole trip. Chills ran down Erik's spine when he stopped to think how happy he was to be back here.

"I don't get it," John said. "What the hell happened over there? Madagascar's got to be a hell of a lot more remote than Decorah. Sounds like your own personal paradise."

"Is the soup hot yet? I'm hungry," he said with a chuckle.

"Shut up and drink your beer. And don't think you're getting off that easy. You were supposed to be over there for two years. And after only what, one year, you bail, and come back to the United States, the most westernized, technologically advanced place on the planet."

"Well, for one thing, I didn't bail. There was a coup-de-etat which forced us to evacuate."

"A coo de what?"

"Coup-de-etat. It's French. It means an overthrow of the government. But to be honest, I couldn't have been happier it happened. It gave me an excuse to get the hell out of there. It might be a lot more remote, but the poverty there is unimaginable. They produce and we consume. They're poor because we're not. I guess I though life in

Madagascar would be less artificial. More down to Earth. But the island's been touched and corrupted by all the forces at work in America. And to top it all off, the only reason I was there was to teach English. Of course I knew that when I volunteered, but I didn't realize I was just helping to westernize Madagascar."

Erik drew a swig from his long-neck bottle.

"What I can't figure out is why we ever invented civilization in the first place," he said after awhile. "It's made a few people very rich and a lot of people very impoverished. We should have stayed in our caves. Why did we have to go and build skyscrapers, churches, cities? Nobody asked me if I wanted to live in a world with all that in it. Just give me the world like it was meant to be. Put everything back the way we found it. I can't think straight with all this noise around me. That's why I signed on to go over there in the first place. I wanted to live in a place where none of that existed. But I don't think that place exists on Earth anymore."

"Then you should come out here more often. And drink another beer," John said, finally ladling soup into their bowls.

The night was suddenly alive with the succulent aroma of spices and canned meat. The intensity of the flavor was a reminder of just how hungry Erik actually was.

"The *pamosavy* legends are just the tip of the iceberg. The stories get weirder the further away from the villages you go. There are stories about witches who sell lightning. I heard one about an American who got into an argument with a local farmer. That night, the American fell asleep with his short-wave radio on his bed. There was a thunderstorm.

Lightning struck the antenna and electrocuted him."

"Fuck! That's some crazy shit. So what about this girl you mentioned? Was she a witch, too? Ellia?"

"I said I'm not drunk enough yet to tell you that story."

John pointed at the cooler. "Ain't gunna drink themselves."

"Suffice it to say I was six thousand miles away from home, lonely, scared, and I escaped into a bad relationship. It was a horrible idea. It ended up alienating me from the people I was over there trying to help—who, by the way, didn't want my help. There was of a growing movement of people who felt the Americans shouldn't even be there at all. The only thing that saved me was the political coup. It was like I was getting early parole for bad behavior. That's when I left."

"Oh, yeah, a political coup. Sure. That's no big deal."

Erik furrowed his brow, trying to figure out if John was going to spin another tall tale or if he was just being sarcastic.

"I was actually just in one of those yesterday," John said.

"Will you at least tell me about *that?* How did it go down?" John asked.

Outside the narrow ring of firelight, night had fallen like a heavy blanket over the river valley. A haze of humidity hung heavily on the air, forming a halo around the moon as thoughts of Madagascar swirled through his head.

"Yeah, that was a pretty interesting day."

Soon the sound of slowly babbling water was the only evidence of the physical world that remained. Before he knew it, his mind was back on the island.

C H A P T E R

3

MADAGASCAR
ONE WEEK EARLIER

"VAZAHA! VAZAHA! VAZAHA!" THE QUICK cadence of the chant buffeted Erik out of an uneasy sleep. The derogatory term for foreigner in the Malagasy language was a word he knew all too well. Specifically, it meant white foreigner. That was the only name the villagers of Ambalavao had for him.

Erik may have been out of favor with the villagers, but what was happening this morning was a new development.

Judging by the faint shafts of light slithering under the poorly-sealed wood shutters, dawn had just broken, and it sounded like a mob had gathered outside his home.

Any sign of animosity from the villagers would be a stark departure from the usual passive-aggressive, silent, doleful stares Erik endured across busy thoroughfares.

Thwunk!

Something hit the shutters.

Thwunk!

Crack!

Not something. Rocks. The mob was throwing stones at his windows.

Shit, this is serious, Erik thought. He sat up in bed and yanked back the thick clump of mosquito netting draped from the stucco ceiling.

More stones. One thud after another.

Then there was a series of evenly spaced hits on the door, louder than all the others. "Erik, let me in!"

Pierre, thank God.

Erik made for the front door in a single bound, just a quick jump across the cold linoleum floor. It was rare that he didn't remember to slip on at least a pair of sandals before getting out of bed, and the temperature on his bare feet surprised him. Not only was the floor cold, but filthy with a thin layer of the red topsoil that blew through the village day and night and defied every effort of sweeping it back outside. The wind always prevailed.

Erik unlatched the door and opened it a crack.

Being the only *Vazaha* in town, he didn't have many Malagasy friends. But Pierre held an office in the local government and was assigned to show Erik around when he first arrived. Pierre liked being in Erik's company to practice his English. Erik was here to teach the language, after all.

"What's got everyone so worked up this morning?" Erik asked in a deadpan voice.

"Erik," Pierre said in his thick Malagasy accent. "The soldiers stormed the presidential palace in the middle of the night. The rebels are finally making their move."

Erik sighed. "And here I thought this was all because I slept with that witch."

"This is no time for joking around, my friend. We just got word over the radio. The airport has been closed, and the international volunteers are leaving the county."

"How are they leaving?"

"By helicopter. From Fianar."

There was an American consulate there. It made sense. The coalition that had been gaining strength the past few months was less friendly to the American presence than the current administration. Among other items on the new political agenda was booting out the Americans.

So this mob of villagers were just run-of-the-mill rebel sympathizers. They'd no doubt prefer to call themselves political activists. How history saw them would hinge on the events of the next few days. Whatever the outcome of the conflict, when the prevailing political winds changed, Erik knew enough to simply get out of the way. That's exactly what the international volunteers were doing.

The current government's rise to power was due in no

small part to its ties to big business interests in the United States. An American-friendly regime had controlled Madagascar for most of the last decade. It looked like today that might change.

"Listen, Erik, I don't think you're in any danger. These people just want to get their town on the new political map of the country. To do that, they need you gone. You'll have to make it to the American consulate in Fianar."

"Thanks, Pierre. But you have a good reputation here and a respectable position. Don't risk that trying to help me."

"Really? What do I have? What's going to happen to me when the new government takes over? All I have for certain is a friend who needs my help. Now. So hurry up. Leave everything. There's no time."

"Thank you," Erik said and reached out to shake his hand.

Strange how things worked out. This new political development was like finding a golden ticket out of the country. Erik couldn't believe how completely things had turned around in just a few days' time. The superstitious Malagasy would no doubt say his luck changed because the rainy season was finally over.

Whatever the reason, Erik knew there was only a small window before that ticket expired. Pierre was right. There was no time to lose.

Not that Erik owned much, but he left it all behind. Books, his short-wave radio, clothes. If he couldn't wear it or fit in his pocket, it stayed.

Erik and Pierre left out the back door, which opened into an outdoor courtyard on Erik's property. The old colonial-style mansion, left over from the French occupation, was owned by the American organization Erik was working with. While the Malagasy families lived in mud huts in the countryside or small wooden homes in the village, the only *Vazaha* lived in a veritable palace compared to the poverty that mired everything around it. Erik marveled at the disparity as he stepped out of the home for the last time.

At the far back of the estate, a tight passageway ran between the exterior of the home and the stone-and-mortar wall around the courtyard. The space between the two walls was narrow and dark, and filled with ankle-deep pools of muddy water. A week ago the sludge would have been twice as deep. The rainy season had been much worse than usual this year.

It was barely wide enough for the two men to walk through single-file, and even the light from the early morning sky found the narrow gap between the walls uncomfortably claustrophobic. They emerged at the far end of the passage, where Erik opened the lock on a wooden gate. In broad daylight, this cranny was bathed in shadow; more so now in the first dim embers of dawn.

The gate closed with a groan behind them, and Erik took care to lock it as much to cover their tracks as to protect the home from crafty marauders.

A century and a half of French occupation had given the Malagasy people good reason to disdain foreigners. That usually translated into passive-aggressive resentment, but there were just as many Malagasy who were shrewd wolves dressed in sheep's clothing. Everyone wanted something.

Erik had quickly learned that a common Malagasy gambit involved cultivating rich *Vazaha*s' trust to get whatever that was.

Schemes to swindle money from *Vazaha*s were endlessly intrepid, though often thinly veiled. Just a month after arriving, Erik and another volunteer who'd been in country much longer than him took a bikeride through the countryside. They were stopped by a man on a motorcycle, who rattled off something in the Malagasy language. Erik didn't know the language well enough to understand, but his friend did. The man was claiming the area they had just entered was a National Park, and asked for their passes to prove they'd paid the entrance fee. It was easier to pay the man off—after Ken negotiated the price down from twenty franks to just five each—than to argue with him. Although Malagasy men usually just wanted money, women were much more dangerous and duplicitous, and it wasn't always obvious what was at stake until it was almost too late.

Ellia came to mind.

"We will go to the taxi bus station," Pierre was saying now, as they walked through the alleyway. Faintly, Erik could still hear the activists' chant fading into the distance.

The few men who passed them in the alley seemed almost oblivious to Erik. He had to side-step one man, bumping into Pierre to get out of his way.

"My friend Jaques can take you to Fianar," Pierre said. "You will have to pay, of course, but you can trust him."

If it meant getting to Fianar, Erik would pay whatever the man wanted.

The taxi station was at the center of town. It was a kludge of potholes, taxis, and a throng of Malagasy people. And everywhere, the ground was a gloppy red mud that caked on Erik's boots and pants.

"Wait here," Pierre said and walked into the fray of people.

Erik squatted at the base of a building, hoping to avoid attracting attention—something that wasn't easy for a *Vazaha*.

Luckily, only a few people cast quizzical stares in his direction. Erik could deal with that. A moment later, worn-out brakes barely halted the momentum of a beat up, rusted out old station wagon careening towards him.

A dark skinned man popped his head out the window, and said only, "*Vazaha*. Fianar. Two hundred."

Two hundred was a ridiculous price. Five times what it should be. Erik didn't care.

A week ago, his rising claustrophobia and panic of being trapped on the island had reached a breaking point. But his two-year commitment made going home out of the question. As unbelievable as the events of today were, now the promise of home was only two hundred francs away. He was fumbling in his pocket for bills when he heard a woman screaming close by, "*Vazaha!*"

Erik was tackled from behind and hit the ground hard.

Money went scattering and a mob swooped in to scoop up the muddy paper currency.

Erik managed to roll onto his back to gain a bit of an advantage, but his stomach dropped down as he stared into the deep, piercing blue eyes of his female assailant, pounding her fists on his chest.

"*Vazaha!*" Ellia wailed. "You take me with you! I come with you!"

Soon there were men that grabbed Ellia roughly by the upper arms and threw her towards the building behind them. A pool of red earth and water splashed up around her as she landed hard. She cowered against the building, not even trying to get back to her feet. Her muddy blue dress bunched most of the way up her mud-caked thighs. With her head in her hands, she made a humiliating sight, though the growing group of men didn't seem to care. The man who had heaved her at the building shouted something at her in Malagasy, and his words were punctuated by some of the other men throwing stones at the cowering, crying girl.

The mob shouted "*Pamosavy!*" at Ellia and now even the incantation of "*Vazaha!*" was starting up again, both chants growing steadily louder and more and more people joined in.

Events had a tendency to spiral out of control quickly around here. The taxi driver obviously thought so too, throwing his station wagon into gear as panic registered on his face. He was ready to peal out of there.

"No," Erik said. "Fianar. Two hundred."

"I can't do it," the driver said. "No *Vazaha*."

Erik heard the unmistakable sound of a gun being cocked. Pierre leaned into the passenger's side window, training a black pistol on the driver.

"You will take him. For one hundred," Pierre said.

"One hundred. Get in the car."

Erik hustled around the back of the cab towards Pierre. Without looking or removing the barrel of his gun, Pierre

said in a thick accent, "You lucky son of a bitch. You go back
to that home you told me about. And when you get there,
you take your raft on that river and you forget about all of
this, you hear me? Get out of this country. Now."

Erik barely heard him. He was distracted by someone
that seemed totally out of place. On the other side of the
lot, where Ellia slumped against the building, a slender,
gray-haired man leaned against the white stucco wall some
distance away from her. He looked as though he didn't have
a care in the world, stocially observing the whole scene,
completely detached from it. What really caught Erik's
attention was that the man was a *Vazaha*—he was white.

"Erik, what are you waiting for? Get in the car!" Pierre
shouted.

His attention came crashing back to the reality before
him. Erik climbed into the back seat, holding a wad of cash
out to the driver. It was more than one hundred. He didn't
care how much more. He just wanted to go home.

The man reached his arm into the back, closed his fist
over the cash and slammed on the gas.

PIERRE WATCHED UNTIL THE TAXI rounded the corner and
disappeared from sight. He concealed his gun in the breast
pocket of his vest, where his long fingers closed over something else, something cold, small and metal.

It had better still be there after all this. The golden key.
The key to Erik's palace. Pierre smiled broadly. His luck
had finally changed.

He walked towards Ellia and slammed his boot into her

ribs, hard. She was the cause of all the bad luck, Erik's, his—the entire village suffered because of her. But now that the rainy season was finally ending, whatever power she had left would soon dry up like the muddy pool she was laying in. No one had to be afraid anymore.

"*Pamosavy*," Pierre cursed her. "Someone had better teach you never to sleep with *Vazahas.*"

He spit on her face, then disappeared into the shadows of the dark alleyway.

C H A P T E R

4

"SHIT," JOHN SAID. "WELL. FUCK. Have another beer," he said, opening one for himself when Erik fell silent.

"I'm just glad I'm back," Erik said, not knowing for sure if he meant the United States, or Decorah, or specifically here, camped on a rocky island in the middle of the Upper Iowa river.

A thick haze permeated the night. Suspended above the river, vapor hovered between the warm water and cool night air, and woodsmoke coiled in a slow-motion dance with fog before ascending to fill in the dark gaps between the stars.

Erik's eyes followed the wisps of smoke from the campfire into the sky. On a clear night, the stars in Decorah seemed nearly as bright as in Madagascar, where there was virtually no light pollution at all.

Erik's academic parents weren't exactly the outdoors-y type, so he was in college before he'd ever seen the Milky Way. They had been lying in sleeping bags in John's backyard one summer. At first, Erik didn't know what he was looking at. Hazy pollution? Fog? It looked like someone had smeared white paint across the center of the sky.

Seeing it for the first time like that was simply eye-opening. Every night since then that Erik spent in a city made him all the more determined to find a different way of life. That was one of the many things that led him to Madagascar.

As if John could sense Erik's thoughts, he said, "You know, you should just move here."

Erik looked over. The same notion hadn't been very far from his own mind. "You have no idea how right you are," Erik agreed.

"I mean you like it up here so much," John said. "You'd get the best of both worlds. Escape to my river whenever the fuck you want, you wouldn't have to worry about the city too much—"

"Believe me, you don't have to convince me."

This was a place the rest of the world had forgotten. It was just the kind of place he didn't think existed anymore.

"Well then just fuckin' do it," John said. "And have another beer."

"Then give me another beer, you think you're so smart."

John took a glass bottle out of the cooler. He dangled it just beyond Erik's reach, holding it around the neck like he had taken a hostage.

"Are you going to tell me about that witch?" John asked, waving the bottle.

"No."

DECORAH, IOWA, POPULATION EIGHT THOUSAND, was not a city without its charms, though an outsider looking in could easily overlook its existence altogether. The city was tucked into a cranny of northeastern Iowa between the breweries of LaCrosse, Wisconsin and the brutally cold winters of Rochester, Minnesota. It was there, built on, in and between a series of limestone bluffs that a small city in Iowa was founded by Norwegian settlers in the early 1850s.

Erik decided to linger in Decorah after the canoe trip. He spent a day just walking around town, taking in the quaint cobblestone streets and the historic downtown. Among its many endearing qualities, Decorah was a town with an appreciation for its own history. Some of its buildings had endured since their original construction, but for the most part, Decorah today was a modern redress of the town's original architecture.

The city was as charming in its simplicity as it was in its contradictions. Despite only one-quarter of its citizens holding bachelors degrees, there were two colleges in the sparsely populated immediate area. The vast majority of locals who held degrees were professors at the colleges and were perceived just as often as not as belonging to an almost entirely separate community.

In many ways, Decorah was not one city, but several,

which, in aggregate, offered a rare and valuable snapshot of American society frozen in time. Shops on Main Street were closed Sundays and every evening except Thursdays, and the ethnic makeup of the town was about as diverse as a lily field. But as homogenous as the area was today, a wide variety of European cultures had initally settled there independently. To this day, relations remained tense between groups who claimed a German heritage and their Hasidic Jewish counterparts. Also stirred into the melting pot was a pervasive Norwegian heritage and a large number of Amish families. An equal number of horse-drawn carriages and F-150's frequented the county roads.

Erik found himself spending hours at the public library, reading about the history of the area and its people, engrossed and fascinated by what he uncovered.

Perhaps not unlike the history of many other places, a small handful of pivotal events had conspired to forge the city into what it was today. Fire had played a major role in the evolution of Decorah. Decades ago, tensions between the Jewish and the German populations had ignited—literally—and a meat-packing plant, a major source of industry and jobs vital to the area, had burned to the ground. The German owners were quick to point fingers at their Hasidic workers.

Earlier still in the area's history, about a century ago, Decorah and its neighboring city, Connover, had been vying for the county seat—that was at least until a fire reduced Connover to ashes overnight, and Decorah was awarded the Winneshiek County seat unopposed. The newspapers were quick to point out that there was not enough evidence to prove arson.

Erik thought his research was simply meant to uncover fascinating facts and help him figure out if this really was the kind of place he could see himself living in. He had been enjoying his time in Decorah, but knew he couldn't impose on his friend John forever. When a whole week came and went, he felt a sense of restlessness. He knew it was time for his vacation to come to an end. He had no idea what would come next.

Wandering around town Sunday morning, mentally preparing himself for the five-hour drive back home, Erik noticed one store downtown bustling with activity. It was a grocery store that locals affectionately referred to as The Granola Bar.

Beginning around the 1970s, Decorah had become a magnet for some burned-out hippie types, and their community within a community had been expanding ever since. Locals referred to them as the granola crowd. No one was really surprised when, before long, they decided it was time to form a co-op, which started out as a simple market that sold organic, locally-grown produce. The co-op expanded considerably from its humble roots into part grocery store, part raw food delicatessen. Little did the owners know that their real claim-to-fame would be their immensely popular smoothie bar, where they offered a wide selection of freshly blended yoghurt and fruit juice concoctions, giving rise to the co-op's new nickname, The Granola Bar, which caught on like wildfire.

On Sundays, it seemed that everyone in town hung out at the co-op whether they were part of the granola crowd or not. People flocked there as much to buy groceries and drink smoothies as simply for want of somewhere to go on a Sunday morning; the co-op was just about the only thing open, not counting the twenty-five churches within walking distance of downtown.

So Erik wasn't too surprised to bump into someone he knew when he walked in. John's mother was a sweet woman with dark auburn hair, and what's more, she was a great cook, which Erik found out when she'd invited him and John over for beef stew earlier in the week. Kim reminded Erik of his own Mom in many ways, right down to her curiosity about his plans for the future.

"Erik! I'm so glad I ran into you! I thought you might have left town already," Kim said. "You know, I was thinking a lot about what you said the other night, about how much you liked it here in Decorah."

Erik suddenly felt embarrassed. He could only imagine where this might be heading. Over dinner, John told his mom about the conversation they had while camping. Erik did like Decorah, it was true, but that was all he was ready to admit to himself at the moment. He had allowed his mind to toy with the notion about what it would be like to live here, but it was nothing more than a pleasant daydream— one of many he was having right now.

"It must feel like someone pulled the rug out from under you," Kim said. "Having to come back from Africa so soon."

"I have to say I'm happy it worked out the way it did,"

Erik said.

"Well, I'm sure it was all part of God's plan for you."
Then, changing gears abruptly, she said, "So, John says
you're thinking about moving to Decorah," while giving
Erik a single soft pat on his upper arm.

That's where Erik was afraid this was going. It felt more
like an accusation than a statement, making him feel vulnerable, as if Kim was laying out the truth for the whole world
to see. And what was the truth Erik didn't want to admit?
That he had no plan for his life, no direction in mind, no
clue what he was going to do next. He felt exposed, naked,
as if he was standing in the middle of the crowded Granola
Bar in his underwear.

Kim sensed his embarrassment, and it made her uncomfortable that she was the cause of it. She waved her hand
in front of her face, indicating she meant nothing by her
comment and Erik should dismiss it. "I'm sorry Erik. The
only reason I mentioned it is that my friend, Marie—she
works at the library—told me you've been spending a lot
of time reading old newspapers the last few days."

Erik was feeling even more exposed now. He didn't realize
spending time at the library counted as news around here.

He flashed Kim a lopsided smile, "Just hoping if I stick
around long enough, it'll make the front page. The headline
could be, Stranger from Chicago likes Decorah. I'd have my
picture in the paper and everything."

Kim laughed, "You never know. That's one thing you
have to get used to around here. Everyone knows everyone else's business. You have to learn not to gossip .... too

much, anyway."

"Why are people gossiping about me?" Erik asked.

"They don't know who you are and they're curious. Anyway, John told me you were teaching English in Africa, and that you have a background in journalism," Kim said.

"That's my whole life's story," Erik said. "Now you know everything."

"Did you know there's a job opening at the newspaper?" Kim asked.

It hit Erik like a ton of bricks. Suddenly his embarrassment softened into a tentative enthusiasm. "Really? What kind of job?"

"Are you interested?" Kim asked.

No one was more surprised than Erik to find that he was, actually, very interested. "Are you kidding?"

"Well, wait right here a minute. Don't go anywhere."

Erik watched Kim walk towards the back of the next isle and exchange words with another woman, who then exchanged words with someone else.

Erik didn't want to know how many people this real-life game of telephone might involve, so he pretended to busy himself with reading the ingredients on a box of organic cereal. But before he had time to read much beyond organic cane sugar, flax seed oil and hemp butter, Kim was standing beside him again.

"Ten o'clock Monday morning," she announced, seeming proud of herself.

"What happens at ten o'clock Monday?" Erik asked.

"Your interview at the newspaper."

"Wow," Erik said. "So that's how people went job hunting before the internet."

He had no idea what the job was exactly, or if he stood any chance of getting it, but he suddenly thought that if this is the way things worked around here, he might actually like living in Decorah.

THE SECOND-STORY OFFICE OF THE jovial, middle-aged publisher of Decorah's twice weekly newspaper carried an unmistakable, heavy scent of cigar smoke. Ken Furman was clearly impressed that Erik knew so much about the history of his little town, and warmed to him almost immediately. The position he interviewed Erik for was Features Editor, which, as it turned out, his qualifications fit like a glove.

"The difference you'll find between working here versus any other newspaper"—Ken said in a deep rumble that sounded like thunder as he conducted the interview in the tabacco-scented office—"is that our newsroom is quiet. Thirty years ago, Erik, I sat in the same chair you're sitting in now. The man who interviewed me was the first publisher of this newspaper. Retired down in Florida now. He warned me I would find this town boring compared to the hustle and bustle of St. Paul."

"What did you say to that?" Erik asked.

Ken laughed, "Well, I says, Frank, I was an intern in Chicago before I ever got paid a dime in Minneapolis. Point is, I've known hustle and bustle in my life, and that's why I appreciate Decorah's newsroom. So Erik, I'm going to give you the same warning Frank gave me back in 1978. Anyone might make a good career for themselves in Chicago or New York, but if you're not a good reporter, you won't last ten minutes in Decorah."

"Why's that?"

"Because if you get lazy in Chicago, a thousand readers might notice, but that's not enough to make you care," Ken said, "but when you get complacent in Decorah, and a hundred of my readers notice, I'm gonna care."

Erik could tell immediately Ken was a man who didn't mince words, and he knew just how to respond to a man like that. "If you're giving me all this advice, does that mean you're giving me a job?"

That produced more thunder from somewhere deep in Ken's gut and he laughed a great belly-roar. "I like you, kid, but I'm not *giving* you a job. I'm warning you: it's yours if you want it."

C H A P T E R

5

PITTER-PATTER. PITTER-PATTER
LEFT, RIGHT, BREATHING FASTER
PITTER-PATTER, PITTER-PATTER

Jogging was Erik Nichim's daily escape. The late afternoon was slowly drawing shadows along the woodchip path as tall silhouettes of pine trees shimmered behind the bright rays of twilight. The unseasonably warm air was thick with humidity, and it seemed as if the hot, sweltering summer would last forever.

Erik liked being able to say that he had run everyplace he'd ever lived. That was Chicago, Iowa City, Iowa, The Netherlands, Madagascar and, for the last three months,

Decoarah, Iowa. It was late September now, and although the trees had already begun to change, the weather hadn't.

In the Malagasy language, the verb for running was *me-kazikazika*. And like so many of his behaviors, *mekazikazika* had drawn stares from just about everyone in Madagascar. Running for recreation was not something people did in a country where almost nobody drove to work, even fewer people had desk jobs, and it was unheard of for anyone to stare at a glowing computer screen for eight to twelve hours every day. Being a newspaper editor meant long hours in front of a computer. Working on a small town newspaper, Erik had many hats, most of them worn sitting behind a desk. The trance of a hard run was something Erik needed to relax, to get out in nature after being cooped up in an office all day. It was a trance in which all the worries of the world seemed to float away.

The metronome of breathing—in-out, in-out—was hypnotic. And the physical activity itself was mesmerizing.

The right side of the brain is used to control the left side of the body, for instance taking a step with the left foot. The left side of the brain is used to take a step with the right foot.

Rapidly switching back and forth, stimulating the right hemisphere, then the left, then the right, over and over, back and forth, again and again, was a simple way to induce a gentle, meditative state. Erik's constant footfalls—left-right, left-right—did just that. He found it extremely relaxing.

Psychologist Francine Shapiro, who studied the brian in the 1980s, developed a technique for hypnosis that she termed "eye movement desensitization and reprocessing" or EMDR, which relied on alternately stimulating the two hemispheres of the brain using pulses of light or sound.

The goal was to alternately distract the hemispheres independently—so the left brain literally didn't know what the right brain was doing.

Her technique was extremely successful for patients needing to relieve anxiety and even recover from post traumatic stress disorder. It was even used to help people stop smoking, or beat other addictions.

Under EMDR, the brain becmes capable of more objectively processing information. It thinks without bias or judgement (the purview of the left hemisphere), and without drowning in a storm of emotion (a product of the right hemisphere).

It's as if both sides of the brain take a nap. In their absence, something else arises—something that remains mostly a mystery to science.

The mind begins to function independently of the brain. Insights that seem hopelessly elusive arise unbidden. But where do they come from? From the elusive *soul of the mind?*

Erik had a tremendous respect for EMDR. The therapy allowed him to step back, take an objective view when he was being treated for anxiety.

He'd tried a number of different things to keep his anxiety at bay—from cooky new age stuff to psuedo-scientific alpha wave therapy. EMDR was the only method that worked. Erik knew the same principle applied when he went running. The hypnotic exercise offered an escape from the claustrophobic prison of his head.

Erik's mind came back momentarily to the present, taking in the pungent scent of vegetation in the sweltering air. The path jogged along a limestone ridge with breathtaking, if dizzying views of the countryside just beyond the outskirts of town. The beauty was breathtaking any way you looked at it, but when Erik saw it with his soul center, goose bumps sprouted on his arms and the back of his neck.

This is why he was here. Serenity. Peace. The rest of the world was forgetting this simplicity more and more with every passing day. Erik refused to fall into the trap of modern life, the lie that assured everyone that what civilization had built was far more important than what it had destroyed.

Of course the lie persisted in Decorah, too. Even here, it lingered with malaise.

"Are you happy here?" Ken asked when he called Erik into his office that afternoon, his three-month anniversary of taking the job.

It was the first time, but not the last, that someone would ask him that question today. He had half been expecting his Mom to ask that when she called him after work, but coming from his boss, the question took Erik by surprise.

"It seemed like you were at first"—Ken said, taking a deep puff on a long cigar, filling the small office with billowing smoke—"but now you seem distracted. Do you remember what I told you about getting complacent the last time you sat in that chair?"

Ken's commanding presence filled the room. Sitting in the cramped office, permeated by the oppressive odor of Ken's cigar, Erik felt claustrophobic.

"I'm not getting complacent," he said. Despite denying allegation aloud, the intensity of Ken's gaze left nowhere for Erik to hide. He couldn't escape confessing the truth to himself.

"Good. Because you haven't been here long enough to sit on your laurels. Listen, I think maybe you just need to get out of Decorah for a couple days. It can get boring here, I'll be the first one to admit that."

Ken had an uncanny intuition, an eerie way of knowing exactly what was going through someone else's mind. When Ken called any of the staff into his office, the running joke was they had an appointment with Dr. Freud.

True to the name, Ken was a cigar aficionado, and his assessments were usually right on the money. Right from the beginning, he had warned Erik that the newsroom was quiet, and Erik soon learned the truth of that. It was one of the most peculiar characteristics about small town reporting. Most newsrooms buzzed like hives. Not here.

If Erik couldn't reach someone by phone, it was even less likely they had e-mail. He'd walk to their house in the evening, knock on the door and get his story with lemonade to wash it down and a slice of blueberry pie, all while sitting in a porch swing.

Maybe Ken was right. Maybe Erik just needed a break from the predictable monotony of life in a small town.

Already he wondered if moving here was the right decision. It was losing its otherworldly appeal. The beauty of this place had always been the standard to which Erik compared every other place he'd lived. As he was learning to call it home, it was slowly losing its dream-like quality. It was a place in the real world, just like any other.

Maybe Erik would always be restless. Maybe he'd just never be happy. He felt like he was floating paralyzed between worlds. Erik remembered reading about fresh water caves that sometimes flowed out into a saltwater sea. Deep underground, the two types of water inevitably meet, but never mix. Saltwater is more dense. Yet there is no sharp, definitive boundary. Rather, something called brackish water forms an amorphous, ever-changing vortex in between. To the naked eye, brackish water appears blurry and distorted, as salt water and fresh water swirl around one another in an endless slow-motion dance, never touching, never completely free from the other. Looking through brackish water is much like seeing your own reflection in a rippled mirror.

Yet there are species of fish that have evolved in these narrow brackish zones. They live their entire lives in a boundary region between two opposing worlds, yet for all they know, the boundary itself is the entire universe.

Erik figured he might get along well with that kind of fish. They'd probably have a lot in common, a whole lot to talk about over a beer .... or perhaps a pint of brackish water.

"I don't think you're going to find the meaning of life in Decorah," his Mom said over the phone that afternoon. "Don't be so hard on yourself. You'll find whatever you're looking for eventually."

"I guess so," Erik said. "It's just really isolated out here, which I like, but it's kind of lonely. That's what's really getting to me."

"Where's your friend, John?"

"He's around, but he's going to school in the evenings. And everyone else seems really cliquey. What was I thinking? Most young people don't move *to* Decorah, they move away from here!"

"Have you been sleeping better at least?" his Mom asked.

"No, I'm still having those nightmares."

"Well, I'm sure it's just the stress of moving to a new place and trying to adjust. Don't worry about it."

Erik didn't much feel like talking about it with his Mom right then, and decided to change to subject. They chatted a bit longer about his parents' book tour and a few other odds and ends before Erik hung up and finally made it out to the woods for a run.

Now, six miles later, the sun was just about to set and his body felt near the point of exhaustion. Maybe it was the heat making him woozy. Or maybe running seven miles a day was just too much.

As much as he loved it, sometimes running was a double-edged sword. The more frequently he ran, the faster, harder and longer he needed to go in order to chase down the elusive runner's high.

He slammed on the breaks suddenly, doubling over, fighting off a feeling of light-headedness and nausea. What he wouldn't give for a tall glass of cold water.

The car was still a mile away. He knew he had to make it or risk passing out. There was no way to call for help and no cell phone service this far from town and so far off the highway.

Still doubled over, but with his heavy panting slowing, Erik began to hear the faint sound of babbling water. He imagined this was exactly how a mirage in the desert would tantalize and tease a desperate wayfarer's senses.

He struck off the main path, into the forest, toward the sound of the water. He was confident he knew these woods well enough not to get lost. Then again, he thought he had traveled them well enough to have come across all the brooks and creeks that cut their paths through the trees. And he didn't know of any fresh water around here—aside from the unattainable river that was more than a hundred feet of sheer rock below.

He wasn't thinking how foolish it might be striking off the path on his own. At the moment, he was actually thinking about his daily trek through the steep countryside in Madagascar to fetch water from the village well. There he had to worry about twisting an ankle over the steep and rocky terrain.

He dodged through prickly pine needles, shading his eyes from blinding swatches of sunlight streaming through the branches, encouraged by the sound of water that was growing louder all the time.

The forest began to thin as he came precariously close to the edge of the bluff. Just feet from where the last tree put down roots, Erik was pleasantly surprised that the forest nestled a ribbony little brook.

Seldom had he seen a more welcoming sight.

He knelt beside the brook and dunked his entire head in the cooling water, then thrashed his soaking hair from side to side before palming his thick, shoulder length mane back over his forehead with a slop of water that ran down his back.

Then he drank deeply, frantically. Each swallow felt like cold hands massaging his throat and chest.

He smiled, just thinking how ridiculous it must look for a grown man to be kneeling beside a stream with as much purpose as a kid at a water park on a scorching summer day.

Someone laughed.

Erik turned. "Who's there?"

The only hint of movement was a squirrel darting from tree to tree. He followed the running water with his eyes until it disappeared deep in the trees. It struck him how crystal clear the water was.

As Erik watched a school of small, rainbow-colored fish fan its way upstream, it looked more and more like he was looking into an aquarium. Ripples on the surface shimmered over a collection of red rocks untouched by algae and dusted with a fine layer of golden sand.

That's when he saw a reflection on the surface that gave him pause. At first he thought it was his own, but it didn't reflect his movements. And the vague outlines and contours of the face didn't look anything like him. The jaw was much softer, the cheeks higher.

The eyes blinked. "Hello," said a female voice.

Has it really come to this? Am I that dehydrated? Or just that lonely that I'm hearing voices?

What had only been a vague outline of features was now remarkably clear. In striking detail, Erik saw the face of a beautiful, young, auburn-haired woman.

Well, if I'm going to have an imaginary friend, at least she's not too hard on the eyes, he thought.

The woman's face seemed to displace all the water around it except a few ripples on her cheeks.

"Hello?" Erik asked, and again threw his glance behind him, still certain there must be someone standing over his shoulder.

Water splashed him in the face.

"I'm over here," the woman's voice seemed unsteady, cracking as though she'd been weeping.

Erik realized those wet spots on her cheeks were tears.

"Have you been crying?" he asked.

But if I'm talking to an imaginary friend, do I really need to talk out loud?

"I'm not imaginary!" she said, getting defensive.

Well, I guess that answers that question, Erik thought. Imaginary people have imaginary minds that can read real people's thoughts. It was all very logical.

"I'm *not* imaginary!" she insisted.

"Sorry," Erik said aloud. He certainly didn't mean to offend her, even if she was .... he stopped himself before thinking the offensive word again.

"Anyway, why are you crying?" Erik asked. Talking out loud made him feel a bit less like he was losing his mind.

"It's my sister," she said.

"Your sister?"

"Claire's dead."

"Oh, I'm sorry....? Do you want to be alone, then?"

"No, stay. Please. I need someone to talk to. Someone from your side. What's your name?"

"Erik."

"I'm Rachel. You remind me of Timothy."

"Who?" Erik asked, more confused than ever. "Why do I remind you of him?"

"Because you don't think I'm a real. Timothy's the old man who thought I was a fish. That was years ago, when I was little."

"You've been here that long? Do you live here?"

"Hold, on! It's my turn to ask a question," Rachel said. "Why are you all out of breath?"

"I was running."

"Was someone chasing you?" there was a tone of concern in Rachel's voice.

Erik laughed. "No, no. I wasn't running *away* from anyone. I was just running. For exercise. You know, *mekazikazika*," Erik said.

"*Mekazikazika*. That's a strange word."

"Yep. Ok. My turn. Are you from Decorah?"

"Where's that?" Rachel asked.

"Decorah. You know, from the city."

"No. I've never been to any of the cities. Actually," her voice was contemplative now, "I've never been anywhere else except the village. Pathetic, isn't it? Not that I'd have any idea where else to go even if I wanted to leave. This place is about as far away from the village as I've ever been on my own. Claire and I have been coming here since we were kids."

When she said *the village*, somehow Erik didn't think she meant the cutesy name of a new subdivision. An image of huts and mud roads popped into his mind.

"It's my turn now," Rachel said. "What's the significance of the those metal pieces on your face?"

Erik had to think about that one for a moment. "You mean my glasses?"

"They're made out of *glass?* They're beautiful!"

"Thanks," Erik said. "My turn?"

"Okay. Do you want to know about my sister?"

"If you feel like talking about her."

Rachel sighed. "She died three days ago. In child birth. This is the last day of her *Rakjal.*"

And before Erik knew it, Rachel was talking a mile a minute, almost rambling, as if she hadn't had anyone to talk to in long time and she was going to tell him everything.

"You know the caves back by the spring?" she asked, "Where the rites are performed every year? Claire was chosen to bear her first child during the rites this year. She was always lucky and I was envious of her. Why wasn't I chosen? I never got anything she did."

That's when Erik noticed something strange—no, everything about this situation was strange. What was truly bizarre was that when Rachel started talking fast, Erik noticed that her lips didn't match up, as if her voice was dubbed in. The whole experience was like watching a movie. His mind kept conjuring up vivid imagery to accompany her words.

"But now I think, what if I *was* chosen?" Rachel continued. "Then maybe my spirit would have left instead of hers, and that really makes me wish it could have been me instead. Claire was always so nice, so nice to everyone."

Erik couldn't begin to know how to respond. But out of everything she just said—most of it making very little sense—the caves she mentioned stuck out to him. She said the caves were by the spring. She must mean Malanaphy Springs, but there weren't any caves back there as far as he knew.

"The caves are by Malanaphy Falls," Rachel's voice said.

The image of a cascading waterfall came to mind, but that hardly described Malanaphy. Even for a spring, it was a modest size.

Wait a minute. That time her lips didn't move at all. And Erik knew he hadn't said anything about Malanaphy out loud. So how could she....

"Rachel, say that again...?"

"I didn't say anything," she said.

He could only reach one logical conclusion: Rachel was definitely a figment of his imagination. It was either that or the brook was a portal into another world.

I'd be crazy to believe that! Erik thought.

Any less crazy than if you believed in an imaginary person? Rachel asked in response. *Besides, I already told you I'm not imaginary.*

"And you're *not* crazy," she added aloud. "It has to do with the magic in the water, but I don't know exactly why. The magic's the reason I came down here today. Well, that and because I thought I wanted to be alone. But I'm glad you showed up. I thought maybe I'd see Claire in the water."

"So, if you are from ... another place ... have you met other people from my world?" Erik asked.

"Just the man with the strange hair when I was a little girl."

Well, that was disturbing.

"Hold on. Are you saying you met a stranger in the woods when you were a little girl? He didn't try to .... do anything .... I mean ... were you scared of him?"

"No. Not at all. He was scared of *me!* He said he didn't realize that anyone except him could control the magic of the brook. I had no idea what he meant. That's right before he jumped in the water after me."

Erik couldn't help but laugh. It all sounded so absurd. The image of mermaids flashing in his mind was even stranger. "Well, don't worry," he quipped. "I won't jump in after you."

That brought an unintended result. The reflection of her brow furrowed, possibly in confusion, but it looked more like she was annoyed at the comment.

"Good. Because it won't work," she said. "We can see each other, but we can't travel between the two sides that easily. Claire and I managed it, but not very well. But if you're nice to me, I'll show you what I *can* do."

Erik didn't say a word. He didn't have time. Before his eyes, a woman began to materialize out of the ripples in the water, at first an extension of the brook, translucent and consisting only of slowly coalescing liquid. Then the apparition took on a quicksilver-like complexion, and finally materialized into a curvaceous though petite female form that appeared to be shrouded behind a blanket of mist. Soft color slowly filled into her skin, but never more than vaguely.

Rachel struck a regal posture, standing slightly over five feet tall. Her slenderness made her seem taller, and the soft curves of her hips were shown to advantage under black pants that clung to her legs. She stood with one hand on her hip, arching her back slightly and laughing coquettishly. A brown leather sash covered her chest, leaving her shoulder blades and navel exposed. Her bare feet were covered with dry, caked mud.

"Impressed?" she asked.

"How did you do that?"

She explained at a mile a minute, which was amusing to watch as she gestured just as quickly with her hands. "I wish I could do better, and I know it can be done, but I haven't figured out how yet, but I think"—pointing an index finger skyward—"Temara knows, but refuses to speak of it, and she forbids me to come down here because she says the magic is too dangerous because the water is a portal to a place we cannot yet remember—actually"—shaking the same index finger like a stick— "come to think of it, that's the same way that the old man described it—a place we cannot yet remember, because I don't think there's a word for that in our language.

"But according to Temara, many generations of Priestesses from all the surrounding villages within a week's journey have known about the brook. But the magic's forbidden because no one knows where it comes from or how it works. But that's simply absurd. I mean"—shrugging, both hands now on her hips— "if you don't understand something, you should try to learn, not run away."

Erik barely slipped in, "I agree."

"So Claire and I always came down here, and that's how we learned just a little bit about how to use the magic. It was always easier to control when we were together. Now that it's just me, it'll be harder."

Erik chuckled under his breath, "Rachel, Rachel, please, slow down. So where do you think the magic comes from?"

She furrowed her brow again, the same as before. Erik thought it could just mean she was trying to process something she wasn't expecting. If the speed at which she spoke was any indication, Erik suspected a diverse assortment of thoughts was constantly racing through her mind. "I really don't know," she said. Then, after considering for a moment, "But I'm sure the man with the strange gray hair does."

"You keep telling me about him."

"I think he found this place by accident, and it scared him. He said he feared that someone would accidentally stumble on his brook, and they were going to drown in it."

"*His* brook?"

"That's what he said. He was right, you know—we did find it by accident. Well, actually, Claire found it first when she left the trail to go exploring. I found her here in the clearing and we both immediately fell in love with this place. It was our secret. No one else knew about it, or so we thought, and we promised we'd never tell anyone. But one day we had to tell Temara."

"Why?"

"She had a vision in the cave that we were in danger—she

was in a Fire Trance and saw us drowning, the same thing the old man said. Temara demanded we tell her where we went when we snuck off. You don't know Temara. We had to tell her. She's a formidable presence."

Erik knew something about feeling compelled by someone with a formidable presence. He remembered how the one-sided conversation with his boss this afternoon had left him feeling about two inches tall.

"Temara forbade us to go back," Rachel said. "That's not to say I always did what I was told. What Temara doesn't know won't hurt her. At first we came here just to play, but then, after awhile, we started to play with the magic...."

It looked like Rachel was raising her hand to her eyes, as if to dry fresh tears, when suddenly and without warning her apparition dissolved before Erik's eyes. Her face once more became just a reflection, suspended somewhere below the crystal clear water and above red rocks set in glittering gold sand on the riverbed.

Erik could clearly make out fresh tears on her cheeks.

"Claire's burial is tonight," Rachel's voice came, less level-headed than before. "The sun's almost gone. I have to go!"

Erik heard heavy footfalls thumping across the ground then fading into silence.

And then only the sound of the slowly churning water remained.

HE COULD FINALLY SEE THE asphalt parking lot, and it was a welcome reminder of the real world.

Seeing the girl at the water was an even stranger thing

to think back on than the experience itself.

It was one thing to experience a break from reality, Erik thought. It was quite another to think back on it after regaining one's senses. He was dehydrated. It was a delusion. The day was a scorcher. A seven-mile run was just too much.

The pitter-patter of his feet finally ended at the yellow post marking the trailhead.

Erik turned to take a look back into the dark woods he had just emerged from, where twilight had almost completely disappeared under the canopy.

There was a flutter of white in the darkness.

Erik's heart pounded in his chest.

Relax! There's nothing there.

A rustling of leaves. A shadow fluttered across the path, chased by the silhouette that appeared to have a human shape.

The old man Rachel talked about?

Listen to yourself! That's absurd! Relax. It wasn't a person. There's no one in those woods. It was probably just a bird in the trees. That's where birds live. In the trees.

Part of him wasn't so sure.

Erik ran to the car and slammed the door closed behind him. He never drove so fast in his life.

C H A P T E R

6

ERIK WAS DISTRACTED AT WORK THE next day. He had thought a big dinner and a good night's sleep would help clear his head. He was out as soon as his head hit the pillow, but woke up just after four in the morning. For untold nights in a row, he'd been having the same nightmare. It had actually been haunting him on and off ever since he'd returned from Madagascar. Ellia was always there. And it was always the same. Except recently, he was having it a lot more.

Erik shuddered at the thought. Sitting at his desk, unable to concentrate on the feature story he was writing, a grin suddenly crept over his face and he let out a soft chuckle.

"What's so funny?"

Erik looked over at Alicia, who sat at the desk beside his. "What's that amused look on your face?" she asked, without interrupting her rhythmic pecking on the keyboard. Alicia was the charming, chatty, sandy-haired woman who worked the news desk. At first her high-pitched voice that seemed to perk up with unbridled enthusiasm about even the most mundane things had annoyed Erik, but it had become, ironically, that very quality that now endeared her to him. He found that he very much enjoyed their midday chats whenever there was downtime in the newsroom. He could count on Alicia to lend an ear if something was bothering him, and she always had an amusing anecdote at the ready to lift his spirits.

"Remember I told you about that dream I keep having?"

Alicia suddenly stopped typing, rolled her chair away from the desk and swivelled to face Erik, propping her chin on her palm, with her elbow resting on a knee. "The one about your ex-girlfriend?" she perked up enthusiastically.

"Yeah, that one."

"Yeah! Did you have it again last night? What do you think it means?"

"I have it every night. I don't know how to interpret it. I was actually just thinking I should ask our psychiatrist what it means."

"Ken? Oh, I'd love to see the look on his face! I don't know, Erik, Ken actually might send you to a real psychiatrist."

"Yeah and he wouldn't know the half of it."

Alicia looked hesitant, "Why? What do you mean?"

"You want to know something really strange?"

"Well ..." she stammered, "that depends. But I'm sure you're going to tell me anyway, so go ahead."

"When I was out running in the woods...."

Where to even begin? Erik thought.

"I saw this woman. And I don't even know how to explain what happened next."

"Ummm, you took her back to your place?"

"No!"

"You mean...Erik!...right there in the woods?"

"No! Skip the part about the woman. But listen, after I talked to her, I swear I saw an old man hiding in the woods. And I think it might be the same guy I saw before."

Alicia drew a long breathy gasp, as though the true gravity of the situation just dawned on her. "Now that *is* creepy. My God, did you tell anybody that you saw a creepy old man in the woods where women go jogging?"

"Who am I going to tell?"

"Oh, I don't know. The cops? Erik! What about that lady you met? You just left her alone with the creepy old man?" Alicia's incredulity was turning into terror for the girl.

She is completely misinterpreting what I'm telling her, Erik thought. But then again, anybody down-to-Earth would probably jump to the same conclusion. After all, how could Erik possibly explain that she only appeared as a mirage in a pool of water ... and then as a translucent spirit, and that the old man was probably just a figment of his imagination, too.

Luckily, Alicia's emotions tended to turn on a dime, and Erik was relieved that her terror suddenly morphed into something else all on its own during the natural course of her monologue. He could almost see the little gears in her mind turning as she considered the story from all possible angles.

"Well," Alicia continued, "he probably saw you, too, so he knows that you know he's there. So hopefully that was enough to scare him off. Erik! It's a good thing you were there! My God! You might have saved that young woman's life! Imagine if no one was there to see that dirty old man! But I'd still report him!"

"Alicia, I don't even know if I saw him. More like I didn't really see him. But I kind of did. But the thing is, like I said, I think I saw him once before. The same old man. In Madagascar."

"Yeah, Erik," Alicia said sarcastically, "you *should* go tell Ken. Ken, when I'm not at work, I spend my time alone in the woods like some creepy old man and fantasize about the young women jogging by. Oh, and when I'm at work, I can't concentrate because I keep having nightmares about my ex-girlfriend. Oh my God, Erik! You are a basket case. You're really losing it!"

"It really sounds that bad, huh?"

"Uh, yeah! Go ask the psychiatrist, see what he says."

"Erik"—the intercom on his desk had suddenly chimed into their conversation with its customary high pitched *beeeeeep* before broadcasting Ken's unmistakably deep baritone—"can you come up to my office, please."

Erik paused. "Uh, sure, Ken."

Then the sound of Ken hanging up his receiver came

through Erik's speakerphone as the intercom went dead again.

Alicia's jaw dropped and she covered her open mouth with her hand and gasped. "That. Was. Wierd." she said. "Do you think he was eavesdropping on us?"

Alicia had a charming way of pausing after each of her first few words for dramatic effect and then finishing her sentence at a mile a minute.

"Maybe he could sense that we were talking about him," Erik jibbed.

Alicia gasped again. "Do you think so? Doo-doo-doo-doo Doo-doo-doo-doo," she hummed a few eerie notes under her breath. "Time to go and see the prophet! Don't forget to tell him about your little freak show in the woods there. And ask him about your dream. My god, you guys are going to have a lot to talk about. I mean, assuming he wasn't eavesdropping the whole time!"

"Wait, why did you call him the prophet?"

"Well I don't know what to call him. The clairvoyant? The oracle?"

"What happened to Dr. Freud?"

"I don't know. It. Is. Bizarre. The things that man knows. No psychiatrist could do that. He must have been listening to our whole conversation! He must have been! Otherwise, how would he know to chime in at exactly that moment? My God, that man's ears must be burning all the time."

ERIK, I SEE A SOLUTION to both our problems," Ken said, raising his left hand to scratch an itch just behind his left ear. "You need to get out of town for a few days. I have a story I need covered. My only concern is, if I send you to Marquette, you might just decide not to come back to Decorah," he said.

"Why are you sending me to Marquette?" Erik asked. "And where is Marquette, anyway?"

"It's a little town in Iowa right on the Mississippi. About an hour from here. The area is known for lots of old Native American burial grounds. These three college guys—one of them is from Decorah, which is why we're covering the story—were walking around the state park, and this is a great quote, listen to this guy. He said, 'it felt like God was blowing on me from underground and he had bad breath.' Oh that's great! We're gonna print that! Well let the schmuck believe it was God if he wants. It was actually stale air from deep underground. These three guys found the entrance to a huge cavern."

Erik almost thought he'd misheard. "They found a cave?"

"Seems to be huge. Might be the biggest ever discovered in Iowa. Some guys from National Geographic are going to be down in Marquette for a couple days. There's going to be a press conference tomorrow, and I want you down there. And then take the weekend for yourself. Get out of Dodge for a few days."

Erik agreed. That did sound like a good idea. "Thanks, Ken. That might be just the thing. You do have a sixth sense about people, don't you?"

"Don't brown nose, kid."

Erik laughed, but Ken's remark barely registered. His mind was reeling with ideas. One in particular stood out.

"Ken, are there any caves you know of down by Malanaphy Springs?"

"Not that I know of. Why?"

Erik brushed his curiosity aside. "Just looking for an angle, that's all."

"Okay, just don't get lost while you're looking," Ken said.

BECAUSE ITS SOURCE WAS TYPICALLY deep underground, spring water was among the coldest water on Earth. So even though Erik didn't know of any, it was certainly possible there were caves around Malanaphy Springs like Rachel said.

If those kids in Marquette could find a cave, what about right here in Decorah? After work, he decided he would do a little exploring. Maybe he would find a cave. Better yet, maybe he could shed a little light on the strange encounter with the woman in the forest yesterday.

Maybe Malanaphy wasn't a spring at all but part of a vast underground river. Explorers had only recently found the world's largest underground river flowing through the world's largest cave in Vietnam. None of it had ever been discovered until 2007. Who knows what else might be out there, right under our feet?

The Hang Son Doong—Mountain River Cave—was almost 3 miles long and its largest chamber had a vaulted ceiling nearly 700 feet tall, and all of that had existed for millions of years, unbeknownst to any human.

Erik knew all of the obscure facts he collected made him come across as kind of a know-it-all. Even in his Features articles, many of his obscure factoids were left on the cutting room floor. What Erik didn't let on to most people though, was that aside from traveling to Madagascar, most of his knowledge was purely academic—a trait he got from his parents, who were both tenured professors. Somehow mentioning to his friends that his parents taught linguistic anthropology didn't help Erik's social life. Linguistic anthropology, the technical term for the study of ancient languages, didn't exactly roll right off the tongue, and wasn't a field most people knew a whole heck of a lot about. The technical term for his entire family, Erik supposed, was bookworm.

But so what? Learning about things like the large cave in Vietnam really gave Erik a sense of perspective. Compared to the vastness of the cosmos, all of human civilization was like a single bacterium growing on the floor of the Mountain River Cave.

Of course, caves like that in Northeast Iowa were probably just a figment of his imagination. And having an active imagination didn't make a person crazy.

Erik remembered how fast he drove home from the trail yesterday. How silly. There was nothing in the woods. Of course, if he really believed that, he wouldn't be here now.

It was getting dark more quickly than he had anticipated, adding to the sense of adventure. Erik switched on his flashlight, but was somewhat disappointed at its feeble offering of light.

I really should turn back, he thought. *I could easily break an ankle out here and no one would find me for days.*

But I've come this far. It'll only take five minutes to make it to the spring from here.

"Shit. I'm talking to myself."

Finally, it came into view. At the next bend in the river, the falling spring water seemed to magically emerge out of the limestone.

The world back here was covered in shadow, with twilight barely filtering through the canopy. Erik was ready to kick himself for not thinking ahead enough to check the batteries in his flashlight. In the eerie light, he thought he could simply step through the spring and disappear, like stepping out of time.

Empty beer cans littering the ground were an unwelcome reminder of the real world. And there, siting on a log at the burned-out campsite, was the gray haired man Erik had seen twice before.

His features were starkly different from what Erik had perceived in his earlier glimpses. This was not an old man at all. His face wore no wrinkles; his flesh was in fact as smooth and unblemished as silk. It was the long, gray hair cascading nearly to his waste that gave the lie to his age. The silver strands seemed to shimmer, reflecting what little light of day still lingered. A jet of black streaked down the center of his metallic mane, lending its likeness to a horse's tail.

In Madagascar, Erik had thought he was a *vazaha* — a white man. He could now tell that presumption had also been rash. He was light skinned, to be sure, but not without pigment—the faintest of copper. The angle of his eyes was slight but discernible. Perhaps he had Native American or

Asian ancestry.

"You," Erik accused.

"Were you expecting someone else?" the man asked.

"I wasn't expecting anybody," Erik said.

"Indeed," he said, raising a bushy gray eyebrow. "So you did have an expectation. Nasty little buggers, aren't they? Manipulative, mischievous, selfish, little gnats. Definitely not to be trusted. I dare say they have a life of their own—and they're only interested in themselves, aren't they—their own survival?

"Think about it," the man continued, "an expectation creeps into your mind. Then it starts trying to convince you it belongs there. Convinces you it's there to help you understand something—something fundamental about the world around you. Next, the expectation encourages rationalizations about other things that support its premise. Soon enough, you believe in your expectation absolutely, and your mind begins to reject any notion that contradicts it. And the expectation thrives. Soon it has taken over, like a virus. And instead of lending you a better understanding of the world, it has subverted your capacity to understand the truth."

Erik could only stare. "Who are you?"

"I am what you expect me to be, of course. At first you saw an elderly man because that's who you believed had gray hair. You also expected me to be Caucasian—because, more than anything, your mind has been conditioned to think primarily in dualities. In a world of Malagasy people, a quick glace gave you only enough information to tell you

I was certainly not Malagasy. Then your mind filled in the gap and told you I must be like you. But why? The truth is, there's a very small strand of latitude on your world where humans like you evolved—ones who possess a genetic mutation for so little pigment in their skin. Yet today, it's the descendants of that relatively small group of people who control the world. They have, shall we say, re-created it in their own image—and done so completely without remorse. That's a bit odd, don't you think? Well, not when you consider that it was their belief, their expectation that 'might meant right' that allowed the minority to feel justified in subjugating the majority—and all of nature. So that's your history in a nutshell. It all comes down to a single, false expectation about the way the world should be. Your people have bleached the world just as your expectations have bleached your mind."

"Do you have a point?" Erik said. "You're giving me a headache. Do you always blather on at such length?"

"My point is that history is a projection of beliefs and expectations that are acted out just as reality is a projection of what your mind expects should be out there. Yet the entire world you expect to see is just one permutation of reality. And as for me, I am so far removed from your expectations that you long ago lost the capacity to comprehend what I truly am. We'll have to expand your horizons a bit first."

"That's a little conceited, don't you think?" Erik said.

The man thundered a great belly roar of laughter. "You're certainly not afraid to speak your mind. That's very commendable, *Kheric.*"

Kherik? The way the old man pronounced his name, with the strong *kh* in front of the vowel, was actually his given name. Erik was just a nickname. Leave it to linguistic anthropologists to pick an ancient word from a dead language for the name of their son. Lucky for him, it sounded a lot like a modern, normal name.

"Why did you call me that?"

"That's your name, isn't it?" The man came to his feet and extended a bony hand. "Nice to meet you."

It was a reflex for Erik to shake it despite his rational mind's desire to resist offering any form of reciprical platitude. It was as if the old man was manipulating him, even in this small gesture.

"Do you know my parents?" he asked. "Have we met before?"

"So many questions. Yes, our paths have crossed, but no I have not met your parents. But I have read their book," the old man said.

"You're probably the only one."

Despite some initial enthusiasm in the weeks following its publication, the book had been a total flop. Their theory, postulating a linguistic and cultural connection between two unlikely ancient civilizations—the Maya and the Ancient Egyptians—was regarded by the academic community as sheer nonsense. Actually, that was a bit of an overstatement. Academics didn't regard the theory at all. Their book was largely ignored. As it turned out, the sci-fi jacket proved apropos.

Kherik was one of many words that appeared in a slightly

altered form in both the Mayan and Egyptian lexicon, and shared a similar meaning. *Kherik* meant 'master of time' in ancient Egypt and 'daykeeper' in the Mayan world. To this day, the modern-day name, Erik, actually carried the meaning 'forever.'

"You don't remember me, of course, Kherik," the old man said. "You suffer from the same affliction as the rest of your species. Cultural amnesia. You can't remember the future any more than you can remember the alternate histories of your own world. The name of the mind-virus is temporal-causal amnesia, or 'the yet unremembered time'—a very unique pathology—an unintentional side effect, really. But don't worry. You, Kherik, you'll find yourself in the yet unremembered time soon enough."

Erik didn't have a clue what the man was talking about, but something finally clicked for him. "Timothy," Erik said.

"Yes? Nice to meet you," and the man extended his bony hand again.

Erik didn't take it this time. "You're the same man Rachel mentioned. She told me your name is Timothy."

"Ah, yes," said the man, retracting his arm, "so you've been there already."

"Been where?"

"Oh, I almost forgot—the thing I came here to tell you. That the caves you're looking for, they don't exist on your world. So you won't find them, even if I lent you my flash-light"—which inexplicably appeared in the old man's hand, and produced a blindingly white light. "A fair sight brighter than yours, I should say. Now, if you'll excuse me, I must be leaving. You should too, or there won't be enough light to see your way back. Here, you're going to need this."

Timothy held out his flashlight and Erik took a half-step back, refusing the gift.

The man's pencil-thin lips spread into a kind of long flat line extending from cheek to cheek. The expression, vaguely resembling a smirk, was clearly meant to acknowledge Erik's rudeness. "Behave yourself, *Kherik*, and we may meet each other again," the man said. "Actually I know we will. We already have."

"And where is it exactly that you're going?" Erik asked. "Do you live here in the woods?" He was remembering his co-worker Alicia's reaction when he told her about the strange man on the forest path.

"If you must know, I'm returning to the caves," the old man said.

In a quick motion, he flicked his flashlight over to Erik. It flew end over end through the air, and Erik squinted painfully when its beam shone in his eyes. He managed to catch it, and when his eyes adjusted back to the darkness, Timothy was nowhere to be seen.

C H A P T E R

7

HER EYES BURNED BLUE LIKE EMBERS dying in the darkness. Framed by a deep raven completion, her cerulean irises were as bewitching as they were rare among her people.

Permeated by the heavy scent of tropical rain, a welcome, cool cross-breeze blew across the dark room. The black night was alive with the scents of the Malagasy countryside, a sickly sweet mixture of wood smoke and pine trees. And heard even over the cavernous echoes of rain lashing the tin roof, the village was never absent the sound of barking, growling dogs.

Erik lay beside Ellia, his back on the mud ground as she loomed over him, supporting herself with an elbow and pinning him under her piercing gaze.

"Do you love me?" she asked in her own language.

Erik tried to think quickly. He said, "For the time being," thinking she wouldn't understand, that she didn't speak English. Somehow that deception was morally more acceptable to him than an outright lie.

A strange look of bewilderment drifted across her face, but it wasn't the look of incomprehension he was used to when he spoke English to the Malagasy people.

The rain beating the room suddenly stopped, and everything around him went dead silent, still. Was it possible she understood? "You speak English, don't you?" he said, in her language.

She didn't answer—not directly, anyway. "I've heard those words before, and I want you to explain them to me. What does it mean, 'the time being?' "

"Well, *mon coeur*," Erik said in his own broken blend of Malagasy and French. "They are words of love. Great love."

"You're lying," she said. "They do not mean that. I know the word 'time.' It means 'when,' yes? And I know the word 'being,' it means a 'person,' yes? You are a being. A person."

"Well, not exactly."

"Yes, exactly," she said. "I know those words. But what is 'the time being?' This makes no sense to me. A person of time?"

"No, it doesn't mean that," Erik said, rolling over onto his back, away from her, where their body heat had not warmed the dank, cold mud. He shivered with the chill. "For the time being means, 'now.' Today. Right now. For the time being,

I'm here with you."

"And we're going to leave Madagascar, one day, yes, Erik? We will be much happier than we can ever be here."

He felt sympathy for her, trapped in the life she'd been born into. But an even stronger wave of claustrophobia confronted him when he realized she thought he was her ticket out.

"Do you know why I sleep with white men?" Ellia asked.

"*Non,*" Erik said. A few months after they'd met, he'd heard the first person refer to her as *pamosavy*, a witch. The evidence against her, apparently, was mainly that she had slept with a lot of *vazahas*, foreigners.

"*Matory avec vazaha i pamosavy! Matory avec vazaha i El-lia!*" the villagers chanted at her. It meant, "Witches sleep with white men! Ellia sleeps with white men!"

"Why do you sleep with white men?" Erik asked.

"When I was a child, I dreamed how I would take a white man for a husband. I know I'm destined to leave this place with him. I've dreamt of this future. But those other white men were not the ones I dreamed of. It was you, my *Vazaha*. It was always you."

Erik tried to change the subject.

"Ellia, why didn't you ever tell me you spoke English? How much do you understand?"

"Only very small," she said in English. "The man without a name learned me."

"Another *Vazaha* you slept with," Erik said. "Where was he from?"

"He never said. He was much older than you. His hair was

far older than his face. He told me he loved me, promised to take me away from here one day, just like in my dream. I haven't seen him since. That was last year. We spent the rainy season together and then he left. He lied to me. He left me here."

Then, like a flash of lighting, Ellia moved faster than Erik thought possible, and before he could react, she lunged on top of him, flipped him on his back and assumed a dominant posture sitting on his chest, holding him down by his wrists.

"You're not going to do the same thing to me," she said. It was a statement, not a question.

Thunder rumbled outside, and suddenly her blue eyes were glowing a fiery red. Her voice was suddenly deeper, gravely, a hoarse whisper, "You don't understand. You can't leave me in Madagascar, Erik. We will always be together. We always have been."

ERIK AWOKE WITH A START, and wiped the cold sweat from his brow, and at first had no idea where he was.

He fumbled around for the light. Still hearing rain, Erik wasn't sure if he was awake. But the gentle pitter-patter was soft outside, not violently landing on the tin roofs of Madagascar. Erik's pulse slowed when he recognized the gentle touch of the cross-breeze whispering through his apartment, the soft sound of it gently pleating the drapes.

A sudden gust blew in, producing several cool droplets of rain against his face. Yesterday's humidity had burned off and Erik shivered as much from the chill as trying to brush off the nightmarish feeling that still lingered.

Sleeping with a student? What was he thinking? She was one of his adult students, but a student nevertheless.

He remembered how the cat-calls of *pamosavy* had turned a dark corner when the rainy season began. The storms and flooding were particularly bad that year, and people needed something to blame. He doubted they knew about Global Warming, and a witch was more convenient anyway.

Ellia felt like a scared animal backed into a corner, and she gave Erik an ultimatum: take her away from here, or she would tell the village they were sleeping together.

The thought of being with her forever, whether it was in Madagascar or back home, felt like a hand clenching around his throat. He started regretting he'd ever come to Madagascar.

Erik didn't believe Ellia would actually follow through on her threat. He told her it would only make things worse. Which it did. The people who believed Ellia simply accused her of casting a spell on Erik.

For his part, Erik endured suspicious glances from the villagers, but the worst of it was a hot sweat fearing that the international coordinators would hear about it. It took the political coup to wake Erik up from the terrible nightmare once and for all.

Erik came to his feet, trying to bring his mind back into the present. The dream had been plaguing him for weeks. The feeling that he was trapped there. A fear he would never be able to leave the island.

But Madagascar was far behind him. Why did his mind keep returning there?

Then something clicked. It had something to do with

Timothy. Erik had finally seen him in the flesh and suddenly it all made sense.

Hair older than his face, Ellia had said. So the old man had been in Madagascar, too. Erik *had* seen him at the taxi station. He had something to do with Ellia.

But who was he?

Erik always believed everything in life happened for a reason. But what was the reason Erik had gone to Madagascar? In the end, after all the trouble there, what was the point of it?

Maybe his dream was trying to tell him something. Maybe Madagascar wasn't completely behind him. It was following him, haunting him. But why? Erik felt something teasing at the edge of his thoughts, nagging at him, like the bigger picture was there, just out of reach. He sensed that all the pieces of a puzzle were laid out before him. If he could just put them together, everything would snap into focus.

He felt like he was standing on a precipice. Something important was staring him right in the face. Either that, or he was just going crazy. Ready to fall off the edge ... or jump off.

He needed to clear his mind. Think straight. Expand his horizons, like the crazy old coot had said.

Erik practiced meditation from time to time, rarely with much success. It was too easy to get distracted.

He had to free his mind from the prison of its thoughts. The old man wasn't completely full of it. There probably was a lot more to reality than the mind was conditioned to comprehend.

Erik remembered when he first returned home, being

bombarded with everything that had been in the news while he was away. He learned that Madagascar wasn't the only place that had experienced floods that year. It had been much worse in Australia, Pakistan and Columbia. Severe weather was in the news so much that it wasn't really news anymore. Hearing about yet another storm made it seem like a slow news day.

The rainy season in Madagascar was worse than ever. If it was the same in so many other places, that couldn't possibly be a coincidence. Yet fifty percent of his fellow Americans thought Global Warming was a political conspiracy.

But while they had been bombarded with news coverage about it, Erik was a step removed. He realized that allowed him to see patterns that were harder for people standing in between all the dots to connect.

That's what Erik needed to do now. Step outside the dots—think outside his thoughts—if he had any chance of seeing the bigger picture.

The closest Erik had ever come to experiencing a meditative state was during a long, hard run. When he was concentrating on only the sound of his breathing, when everything else drifted away, when he became something separate from the real world.

That's what he needed to do to clear his mind.

The dream was still with him, his mind was racing and he'd have to wake up in three hours anyway to leave for the news conference in Marquette. Sleep was a lost cause.

So he laced up his shoes and went for a run.

At three a.m., Erik Nichim found himself running down deserted, dimly lit streets of Decorah, Iowa, but only vaguely aware of it.

The numinous night was possessed by an ethereal quality. The only light, a velvety man-made blue, illuminated droplets of mist swirling together in waves that formed a soupy fog and a halo around the streetlamps. Erik looked up into a warm mist of softly backlit droplets. The soupy air was encircled in countless crowns, pools of dance partners highlighted with halos under every streetlight.

The earthy smell permeating the air enshrouded Erik in an embrace of the natural world that pierced through the signs of human civilization surrounding him.

So many distractions in the hustle-and-bustle of daily life made such moments of at-one-ment with the universe few and far between.

If Erik could only run fast enough, he could leave everything behind—his life in Decorah, the horrible nightmares, the strange encounters or hallucinations he had in the woods. He could leave behind the feeling that he was simply going crazy.

If he could just run fast enough.

So he ran. Faster.

The fog grew thicker. Erik imagined his mind going blank, fading to white. He concentrated on his breath, heard the soothing, mesmerizing left-right, pitter-patter of his footfalls.

Faster. Faster.

Pitter-patter.

Consciousness flowed like a stream, thoughts rising and

silently falling away.

A realization arose unbidden. All this time, his mind had been analyzing, judging everything that had been happened. The girl in the woods. If she was real she would have to be from another world. That was illogical, therefore, the girl couldn't exist. If she didn't exist, Erik had been hallucinating, which meant Erik was crazy.

So?

Maybe he was crazy. And maybe another world did exist. Erik's logical mind and his emotions had been running circles around each other, both grasping for control.

And his dream. It gave rise to fear and claustrophobia.

Instead of fighting for control, grasping to understand, what if he simply allowed himself to accept it?

Relax and accept.

Left-right. Pitter-patter.

Relax and accept.

If I open myself to every experience—every possibility without exception, without judgement or second-guesses. To see the world with the soul-center of my mind.

It was an intoxicating perspective. Freedom, pure and absolute. Freedom from thought, from fear. Freedom from the prison of thought.

The fog was everywhere now, like a thick coat of white paint on the walls of the world. The rain-soaked cobblestones, the blue velvet of night—it was now almost impossible to pick out any structures though the fog. Like ancient ruins being reclaimed by the jungle, the final remnants of the man-made world became indistinguishable.

Erik was consumed in a translucent cloud. Beyond the translucence there was only more vapor.

The world had dissolved.

Yet Erik's legs were still taking rhythmic steps.

Left-right. Pitter-patter.

A sense of calm washed over him. He could stop running at last.

"You'll fall back into time if you stop now. And it's a long way down."

A human form began to coalesce out of the thick white mist. The black-streaked white mane of hair pulled behind his back, Timothy's pencil-thin lips curled in a smile.

"You," Erik said, this time not as surprised as the last. "Where are we?"

"Right now? Nowhere. We are outside the chronosverse. Free. We have world enough and time. And yet we are expected back imminently."

Timothy picked up his pace smartly, beginning a sprint to some undefined finish line.

Erik was surprised to find that keeping pace with the man was a struggle. His young, fit body, accustomed to daily exercise, was panting and perspiring to keep pace in this void of worldlessness.

Timothy was pulling further ahead, the outline of his body growing ever fainter behind the colorless veil.

Erik wondered if Ken was right after all. That he wouldn't be returning to Decorah—especially if he fell too far behind and became cocooned in the mist.

II

SEAMS OF TIME

C H A P T E R

8

RACHEL COULDN'T CONTROL HER TEARS, AND she didn't want the rest of her clan to see her so vulnerable. So instead of heading home from the brook, she climbed the winding path up the bluff where she watched the sun slowly merge with the horizon.

It was a beautiful affair of crimson and pink with splashes of orange fringing golden clouds in a pastel blue sky sweeping over the sprawling pine forest that blanketed the valley below. Somewhere down there, hidden by a magic she didn't understand, was the secluded grove she had just come from, the one she and Claire had discovered all those years ago.

Rachel had been in her twelfth summer when they first

came upon the brook. She was twice that age now.

The magical place seemed like something out of a fairy-tale, enchanted and irresistible for two young girls with their imaginations.

They would pretend it was a gateway to another world, an enchanted world with technology and huge cities, like the old legends told of.

Little did they realize how right they were.

It was two years later when they met the old man, and he told them the brook really was a portal. Rachel had no idea where to, and the old man wouldn't say, but she didn't really believe all those stories about the lost world of technology.

Rachel could count on one hand the number of times they saw the old man down there, and she remembered the last time like it was yesterday. That was one of only two times she remembered being frightened at the brook. Otherwise the magic had always felt peaceful somehow, soothing.

But that day was different. It was very early morning, just before dawn, when Claire woke her up, telling her she had a bad dream.

"It was about the old man," her sister said. "He was scared. And it was making me scared. There's something I need to know. Rachel, will you come to the brook with me?"

"Right now?"

"IN MY DREAM, EVERYTHING WAS covered in a white blanket," Claire said a short time later on their early-morning hike up the hillside. "I know we were at the brook, but we couldn't see anything."

"My dreams are like that, too, sometimes," Rachel said. "Like my mind just doesn't fill in all the details."

"Yeah, kind of, not exactly," Claire said. "I don't know how to describe it. I just can't shake that creepy, bad-dream feeling."

They walked through the tall grass, wet with early morning dew that soaked through their sandals and leggings. It was about a mile to the brook, and uphill most of the way.

The blue shroud of predawn light was slowly being pierced by the golden promise of a new day. The sun had already emerged from the horizon, but it would be another half hand of time before it would shine into the valley.

The pine trees thickened steadily as the land rose, and when they came to the first clearing, looking back upon the village in the valley far below, they could barely make out the tops of houses below a thick sheet of mist.

"That white blanket over everything .... it was fog," Claire said.

By the time they reached the brook just as the sun was casting its first rays, the fog had thickened considerably. Usually the sun would burn off the mist.

But today was different. Rachel could barely see her sister walking ten paces in front of her. Suddenly, Claire stopped, and Rachel almost walked right into her.

"What?" Rachel asked.

"We have to wait for something."

"Wait for what?"

"For the old man."

Rachel knew better than to ask questions or try to dissuade her sister when she set her mind to something.

So Rachel sat down on a rather uncomfortably shaped rock and waited. "Well this is exciting," she said.

When her behind was just as sore from the rock as her feet had been from the walk, she walked down to the water, and hummed a song to herself as she skipped along the shore.

"*At my back I always hear*
My chariot coming near.
And now before me lies
The palace of eternities."

"Rachel, be quiet!" Claire whispered sharply and tugged on her sister's arm to pull her to the ground. "Look."

She pointed a short distance away through the trees. A short, quick burst of red light illuminated the fog. A strong, soundless concussion to the air vibrated the ground.

Rachel saw two people, a man and a woman, judging from the shape of their bodies. They were running fast, cutting through the mist.

Then, suddenly, their heavy footsteps vanished.

But the silence didn't hold for long. Emerging from the white fog, his breathing labored, there was the old man, Timothy. He looked like he'd been running after the others, but came to an abrupt halt now.

Behind him, there was a dark woman. Rachel had never seen anyone who looked like that before. No one had that color skin.

Timothy's face, too, was much different than before. Gone was the look of wonderment and not-a-care-in-the-world she had come to associate with the old man. It was replaced with a furrowed brow and tightly pursed lips. He glared into the woods where the others had vanished.

Then Timothy looked directly at Rachel and her sister and, as if he was another person entirely, his expression changed instantly back to the one she'd always seen on him.

"Well hello there," Timothy said. "I was hoping I'd catch up with you here."

That was more than ten years ago now. They returned to the brook only a handful of times after that. It wasn't long after when they crossed into the other world completely and, for a few terrifying moments, had been scared to death they would be trapped on the other side forever, that they would never see home again.

Those two frightening experiences, were enough to keep them away. Rachel and her sister were growing older, too, and began passing more of their free time chasing after young men in the village.

Today was Rachel's first trip back in more than five years. It was the only place she could think to go. It was somewhere secluded, somewhere she could be alone with the memory of her sister. Maybe, dare she even think it, to see Claire again? Who knew how the powerful magic worked? What was to say it didn't have power over life and death?

But she didn't see Claire that afternoon. So she sat there, sad and alone with with her brooding thoughts until Erik's reflection appeared in the water.

All those years, the old man was the only one they'd ever seen. And only a handful of times at that. Until today. Now there was someone else from the other side.

It certainly seemed as if the magic had been getting stronger over the years. If that were true, what was causing it? What was the source of the power that allowed the water to act like a mirror to another place? And where was that place?

When Rachel was a child, she didn't ask those kinds of questions. It was a mirror to another place, and that's all there was to it.

Older now, she tried to imagine what her reaction would be today if one of the children told her they'd found a magic river that reflected another world.

She'd probably laugh and chalk it up to an overactive imagination.

But Rachel had simply accepted it when she was a child.

Where was the other world? What was it like? She should have asked Erik. By the goddess, she had a million questions for him.

If only Claire had been there with her. Claire would have known the right questions to ask, instead of letting Rachel just ramble on.

Although Claire was the younger one, she always carried herself with such grace, such maturity.

Tilting her head back to the sky and feeling the soft spring breeze play with her unkempt hair, Rachel vowed then and there to learn all the secrets of whatever ancient magic the brook possessed. It would be her way of honoring her sister. Claire had led her to the grove. Rachel would make it her life's work to learn its secrets.

Lost in her thoughts, Rachel had almost no memory of picking her way down the steep switchbacks that wound down the hillside. When the real world beaconed her mind back, she found herself more than halfway down into the lush valley of hardwood trees.

This was the last overlook the trail offered before its final descent, a steep straightaway to the bottom. Rachel wondered what caused her mind to snap back to reality so suddenly. Maybe it was awareness that picking her way down this last part was not something to be done by instinct alone. A wrong step here, a jagged stone there and she could easily twist an ankle or worse. Pay attention, Rachel, she chided herself.

At the overlook, a jut of the path that offered a sweeping vista, the sunlight cast a sharp meridian across the spikes of green spruce trees that spread across the valley. The green needles and brown branches that peeked their head above the meandering line of the earth's hilly shadow were bathed in resplendent golden light. Below the shadows, the forest and valley was painted in indigo shadows.

Somewhere, in a clearing of trees where night had already fallen, sat the small collection of homes that made up her village.

Just in front of her now, where her path itself passed through the meridian of twilight, Rachel suddenly saw what it was that had snapped her mind back to attention.

Out of the darkness came a voice.

"Keeping secrets, are we?"

Rachel threw a hand over her beating heart as the woman's

silhouette coalesced out of shadows. Temara, the clan's Priestess, stepped into the faltering daylight.

"I've never been fond of secrets, myself. Especially my own. Back in my childhood home, I had a secret place I ran away to, just like you."

Temara was not born into the clan, but had traveled here from a great distance. It was only on very rare occasions that she spoke of her old life. The Priestess was still young in years, perhaps no more than a dozen summers older than Rachel, though her coarse, earthen-brown hair was already discolored by veins of grey. She cut an imposing figure, as broad of shoulder as any man, and wide enough in the hips to bear a dozen children, though she'd never carried one to term. The hard creases on her face had the effect of toughening the leathery appearance of her flesh. From her rough skin to her purposeful, long strides, everything about Temara was evidence of her strong, forceful demeanor.

"When boys started distracting you and Claire," Temara intoned, "I had hoped that would prove enough of a preoccupation that you simply wouldn't have time for childish things anymore," Temara said. "And for awhile, it was. Boys offered you a better reason to stay away from this place than any warning I could ever hope to give you."

She knew. Temara knew Rachel and Claire had been coming to the brook all these years. She had always known. Rachel stood in shock, unable to speak, held frozen in Temara's piercing gaze.

"But no young man could hope to keep your interest forever, could he?"

Rachel could feel it now. Why so many of the clansmen and women were frightened of Temara. Rachel had always thought of the Priestess as someone worthy of respect more than fear. But now, Temara's piercing eyes were peering right into Rachel's soul, seeing all the secrets she held and thought were safe.

"Let's walk together, little one," Temara said.

At that very moment, Rachel didn't even mind being called little one, though she usually felt it was demeaning. All she felt was relief. As long as this conversation took place while they walked back to the village, Temara couldn't keep Rachel fixed in her piercing gaze.

"There's something a lot more interesting than boys, isn't there."

It was a statement. Not an accusation. Not a question.

"Magic," Temara said. She let the word sink in for a long, silent moment, and then said, "So, what was his name?"

"Who?"

"The being from the yet unremembered time you met at the brook."

"Erik," Rachel said. "But he didn't seem like a magical being or anything to me. I don't know who he was or where he came from, but he seemed like just another young man."

"Don't let his age deceive you, child. Beings from the yet unremembered world don't walk though time the way we do. They live outside of it."

Rachel didn't know what to say to that. She was silent for a long time, and grateful they were almost upon the clearing. At the far side was their village.

Rachel tried to maintain her composure, tried hard to hide how every inch of her body felt like it was quaking in Temara's presence. She couldn't wait to be home, even though that meant her sister's rites would soon begin. The rites were supposed to mark the end to the three days of mourning after someone's death. But she knew no ritual could magically make her feel alright.

"After the Dance of Light is concluded," the Priestess said, "I wish you to join us in the caves."

Join the clan of the Priestess in the caves? And after a Dance of Light, no less? Rachel felt a tremendous wave of fear, panic and excitement crash down on her.

There was no night more holy for the clan than one in which a soul passed through the boundary between death and rebirth.

CHAPTER

9

JOINED TOGETHER HOLDING HANDS, THE ENTIRE clan stood in a circle, forming the Ring of Light around Claire's funeral pyre. The Priestess Temara stood alone in the center of the ring, beside the pyre, arms outstretched and hands clasped together above her head, as she led the clan in the traditional benediction.

The deep rumbling of voices chanting together seemed to vibrate through the very ground Rachel stood on. She could feel the words of the prayer flow through her body, ebbing with power.

The way the thunderous chant resonated with the land itself was a manifestation of the power that the Priestess taught flowed through the Veins of Earth at all times. That power was supposedly strong enough to transcend the veil between life and death. Tapping into that power through prayer was the only way to ensure rebirth.

Rachel knew the words of the prayer by heart, but not their meaning. They were in the High language, which only Priestesses learned.

When the chant ended, the night fell suddenly silent, and the earth below her feet grew still. The clansmen and women looked up to the sky. The idea was for all of their eyes to be turned towards heaven at the moment the spirit was committed into the afterlife with the goddess.

In the darkness, Rachel noticed how bright the stars were, draped like a thin sheet of cotton over the night sky, in some places more translucent, in others as white as snow.

She knew what came next: the soft footsteps of someone entering the circle and joining Temara in the center. Rachel thought it was probably Berenice, first servant of the Priestess, who carried the torch that would ignite the pyre. But she would never know for sure. Nights of death were nameless. Every member of the clan was garbed in similar attire, free-flowing black, hooded robes offering anonymity. Rachel was sweating profusely through the heavy wool on such a humid night.

Like a gust of wind, she heard the flames take their first, deep breath as the torch touched the pyre. She was glad she didn't have to watch the wood ignite and send its flames climbing the trellis of wood and bramble towards Claire's body. She felt only the blast of heat surge through her, making an already uncomfortable night even warmer.

All Rachel saw was a soft orange haze ascending from the lower half of her vision. The warm, flickering light blossomed ever brighter until the pure white light from all but the brightest stars in heaven were drowned in its glare.

"Her death is not in vain," Temara had concluded the rite, and was again speaking in the common language. "Jendaer will give birth before the next moon. We now know whose soul will breathe life into the child. Into your graces, our goddess, do we commit this spirit, whose name, in this life, was Claire.

"Claire, be at peace in the Moment, in the Now,
and throughout all unremembered time.
As it is for the living, and the goddess,
from one soul to the next...."

A deep rumble echoed back, "From one soul to the next."

Rachel couldn't hold back her tears.

Her people's ancient beliefs taught that the magic of the goddess flowed most powerfully on nights like this. With the entire clan of the Unfesi joined together in the Ring of Light, Rachel was supposed to be able to feel that power flowing through her body, through the Earth below her feet; feel at-one-ment with the goddess.

All Rachel felt was emptiness. Her sister was dead. It was almost enough to make her disavow everything she'd been taught. There was no magic on nights of death. There was no at-one-ment with the goddess. There was just the feeling of being completely alone, knowing that someone she had loved more than her own life was gone from this world forever.

Rachel thought her crying would sound as loud as thunder in the still and somber night. No one else made a sound. She felt ashamed of her tears as if the others would be able to read her thoughts, her indignation, her selfless desire to cast off all the sacred beliefs of her ancestors so she could be left alone with her misery and anger at her sister's death.

Temara struck out the single beat on the gong that broke the Circle of Light. It was now safe for the clan to remove their eyes from the goddess. Although the pyre still burned brilliantly, Claire's spirit had departed.

The time for somber mourning had ended. The clan's members broke the circle and the Dance of Light began as the drums started beating out a quickening cadence.

Rachel's mother knelt down beside her daughter and clasped her hand in both of hers. "Don't mourn, my child. Her soul will be reborn."

"No, Claire is gone."

Her mother took Rachel's head in her arms, like she used to when she was a child. "Feel the magic of the land. Let it flow through you. It will heal your sadness."

That sounded like something the Priestess would say, and right now, it was not something Rachel wanted to hear. She felt completely alone, and took no solace in the ancient beliefs.

And she was having doubts about Temara's summons to the caves tonight. For a fleeting moment, she considered not going.

Rachel broke away from her mother's embrace, and said,

"Temara asked me to join her tonight, Mother."

A look came over her mother's face, one that Rachel couldn't quite identify, but thought it vaguely resembled sadness. Why would she be sad? Being summoned by the Priestess, tonight of all nights, would be seen by the entire clan as one of the highest honors a young woman could hope for. It hadn't escaped Rachel's notice how Temara had always taken a much greater interest in her than any of the other girls.

After a long pause, holding her daughter's eyes in a firm gaze, Rachel's mother said, "If she asks for you, then you must go."

THE SOUND OF THE DRUMS carried deep into the night as Rachel walked away from the center of the village and the Dance of Light. She stopped by her home to change out of the heavy wool robe that itched all over.

The caves were in the opposite direction of her home, outside the village. Temara, Berenice and the others would be waiting for her there already.

Rachel walked down the village walkways paved with bricks of porous limestone, past the common buildings used in the winter for working, cooking, and eating, past the row of homes that lined the thoroughfare. Just beyond the last small collection of structures, the row of evenly spaced lanterns hanging on waist-high polls along the streets ended, and the light from Rachel's torch took over.

She could have brought her own lantern; the special, slow burning oil was much less crude than this nasty torch, and while a lantern's self- contained flame and polished mirror inside would have shone a far brighter, more focused light to guide her, it would have done next to nothing to ward away any predators skulking in the darkness.

Not that the threat of danger was great on this path. Animals, like the villagers, seemed to have an instinctive apprehension of the limestone walkway that snaked through the dark forest towards the sacred caves.

The sound of drums was receding now, but not yet silent; rather, it blended almost seamlessly with the rushing cascade of water from Malanaphy Falls just ahead. From its birthplace at a small, inconspicuous spring at the top of the limestone bluff, the cold spring water fed into the sacred river and together, tumbled over the hundred foot cliff. Atop the bluff was the sacred clearing where the clan celebrated the solstice and equinox of each season.

As the forest cleared and the spray of the waterfall touched her face, Rachel could see a rising half-moon cast its light onto the waterfall. It cast a spotlight directly on the falls, forming a colorless rainbow in the frothy mist.

A moon bow, or white rainbow, was rare. It would surely be interpreted as an omen by Temara and the others.

"So good of you not to keep us waiting," Temara's voice rose into the night, barely audible over the thundering water.

Rachel was so entranced by the moon bow that she hadn't noticed a dozen women standing at the rocky base of the falls. The dark stone walkway at their feet glistened in the moonlight as Rachel approached slowly, minding every step over the slippery rock.

When she reached the women, they all fell in line, walking behind Temara, who led them into the small cranny between the waterfall and the cliff face. The narrow walkway, barely wide enough for both feet, disappeared into a mouth of blackness protected from view by the falls.

All but the Priestess herself, and the dozen women of her fold, were forbidden from stepping foot back here. Rachel felt a fresh wave of trepidation course through her.

She had never imagined the caverns were so expansive. Taking up the rear of the line of women, Rachel found herself consumed in a vast labyrinth of dank stone walls in a narrow passageway that descended with an even grade down into the earth.

In her mind's eye, she always imagined the clan met in broad daylight.

They proceeded slowly through the narrow passageways, the light of a dozen torches guiding their way. Though the corridor was a winding labyrinth of twists and turns and sharp corners, they never once came to a fork in the road. There were no alternate passageways to take. At least that made Rachel feel better, knowing that whatever happened, she could find her own way out of here if need be.

Finally they came to the end of their journey.

They entered into a large vaulted chamber, the like of which Rachel had never imagined could exist this deep underground. There was no visible ceiling to the chamber other than a void of darkness. They were inside the huge limestone bluff that Malanaphy Falls tumbled over.

The light of their torches cast an orange hue into the

chamber, bouncing off a semi-circle of stone that formed the wall though which they had entered. Beyond the reach of the firelight they brought with them, a soft blue color born right here in this underground universe engulfed the cavern.

The chamber extended as far out before them as the eye could see. The small region of solid earth they stood on, made of sandstone, only existed for perhaps fifty feet beyond the entrance way. Beyond that, where the ground fell away, was the source of the phosphorescent light permeating this mysterious underground world. A vast subterranean lake extended endlessly into the distance. The water seemed to glow from beneath.

Stalagmites of black stone breached the water's surface here and there, while a dense collection of stalactites extended their bony arms down to greet them, some hovering mere centimeters above water's surface. In places, stalagmites and stalactites touched, forming impossibly thin columns. The blue glow from the lake gently caressed every pillar.

In the stillness, a single drop of water disturbed the utterly calm lake and produced an inordinately loud echo.

One by one, each woman extinguished her torch. Rachel felt a hand rip hers from her grasp, and she watched as a woman dipped the fire into the blue water, producing a sharp hiss as her torch was the last to go out.

The blue phosphorescent glow seemed to grow brighter as soon as the last of the light from the world above was vanquished.

The women seated themselves in a circle on the sandy

ground around an iron fire ring filled with wood. Backs straight, legs crossed and palms turned up in their laps, the women closed their eyes, as if beginning a mediation.

Rachel assumed the same posture, but kept her eyes open, watching Temara's every move.

The Priestess placed her hands above the fire pit, and flames immediately roared to life.

The fire crackled as Rachel watched airy smoke waft upwards and disappear into the darkness overhead.

In the silence, Rachel heard the sound of soft, whistling wind coming from some nameless place overhead. It sounded like whispering voices, and gave Rachel the chills.

"Tonight we watched as the flames consumed the body of our beloved sister, Claire," Temara began to intone, "and we celebrated her life and felt sadness at her death. The men drank the fermented grain and will soon be asleep under its spell, leaving us to continue the work of the goddess."

The Priestess cast her eyes on Rachel and then on each of the women gathered in the cavern.

Rachel had known every one of the women her entire life. She had helped them in doing the work of the village, weaving cloth, collecting herbs, cooking meals. Yet tonight they all looked like strangers to her.

All eyes were locked on Temara. She continued, her tone somber, ominous. "Sisters, tonight we welcome Rachel among us. For most of you, it took many years of training and discipline to prove yourselves worthy of the honor of joining your Priestess in the sacred heart of the earth. The decision to invite Rachel here tonight was not a casual one.

Make no mistake, she has proved herself, too.

"Tonight is no ordinary night. Sisters, since the beginning, we have always known there is more to this existence than we realize. And we have long dreamed of freeing the mind to explore the rest of it. We dreamt of a time that all knowledge of work and hardship would be forgotten and no longer burdensome to our bodies.

"There is a gateway to a realm where our minds may achieve exactly that. For many years now, I have allowed the seed of this knowledge to grow without interference. But today, events were set into motion that will change the course of our people's destiny for all time.

"Rachel made contact with a being from the yet unremembered world from which I speak. His name is Erik. I believe this is an intricate part of the goddess' plan to lead us beyond the known boundaries of existence."

Rachel couldn't believe what she was hearing. Temara, in a secret council gathered in the bowels of the Earth, was confirming the brook was a portal into another world.

Rachel was familiar with some of the stories that had been passed down from their ancestors—the ones who once spoke the High language. But those were just stories, fairy tales. Was Temara saying all the myths from the yet unremembered world were true? Who was she to question the Priestess, but that was ridiculous. Was Temara saying all the things in those stories were also real? Electricity? Skyscrapers? Computers?

The list was endless. Every fable she'd ever heard seemed to have some device more magical and powerful that the last.

Whatever he was, Rachel knew Erik was not a member of a lost civilization with advanced technology. That was just absurd. Wasn't it?

Temara set an earthenware bowl on the rough, sandy ground before her. "An offering of earth to the goddess. May our gifts be well received and may she join us on our quest this evening." Temara reached into the bowl and extracted a small pinch of powder, which she flicked into the fire. Green sparks erupted from the flames.

Temara reached over for a small chalice, filled to the brim with some kind of liquid. She sprinkled a pinch of the powder into the cup, and stirred with her little finger.

She took a drink then passed it to her left, and resumed speaking in her lilting, mesmerizing cadence.

"Tonight the magic flows strong from the earth. I can feel it through my body. It has been over a decade since we last embarked on this quest. Although the magic flowed strongly then, as now, I knew the goddess was not smiling upon us at that time. The goddess had come only to tell me that I would soon become Priestess. Tonight, the magic of the earth flows again as it once more delivers a soul to the goddess. Let its sacrifice not be in vain. On this night of powerful omens, we know that you, goddess, have summoned us to embark upon our quest once more. Smile on us this night...."

As she spoke, each of the women drank from the chalice and passed it on. When it came to her, Rachel looked into the thick, brown liquid for a long moment, deciding if she should drink or not. It was too dark to see what it was.

Rachel had always trusted the Priestess, but tonight had given her good reason to question a lot of things she'd taken for granted most of her life.

Swallowing her apprehension, Rachel decided she had no choice but to drink from the chalice, but she didn't know how much of the liquid to take. She decided to err on the side of caution and took a very small sip. When she turned to pass the goblet on, she found an outstretched hand already eagerly waiting to receive it, motioning with its fingers for Rachel to hand it over quickly.

The liquid Rachel held in her mouth felt gritty, but had no real flavor. Closing her eyes, she swallowed.

She knew immediately she had drunk enough. A sense of calmness and peace washed though her body. Her legs felt suddenly weightless, then her arms, then her head, and soon she was blissfully unaware of her entire body. She wanted to laugh at how wondrous the sensation felt, but worried that making a sound would break the trance. It didn't. Rachel became aware of a moan of pleasure escaping through her lips. But not *her* lips. She was out of control of her body entirely, feeling as though she was simply a passenger in a vessel.

With no longer any physical sensation to serve as a distraction, she suddenly became vibrantly aware of a whole new set of sensations.

She felt immersed in the moment, in the now, as if time had slowed to an imperceptible crawl, as if a single moment of time had solidified around her like amber encasing a mosquito. She was wrapped up in a soft, fuzzy blanket of timelessness.

Temara's voice came again, this time accompanied by hard, trembling echoes. "Being of time whom many of us have seen in our dreams, being of time from the as yet unremembered chronosverse, we call on you now. Appear before us."

Silence filled the cave, broken only by the sounds of the crackling fire. Time was immeasurable, dragging out into a long, pleasurable sweep, like flowing water.

The wondrous, floating feeling intensified in Rachel's body. Opening her eyes and daring to peek out from her cocoon into the fire-lit cave was a pleasure all its own. She found herself mesmerized by the green fireflies dancing around the lapping fire.

She couldn't look away. The vibrant colors entranced her. She felt the kind of giddy excitement she hadn't known since she was a child.

The tongues of flame grew taller and then coalesced into two pillars, which soon took on human forms. The bodies remained very pallid in color, but Rachel recognized both of them. Erik was the younger one, and Timothy was the older, thinner, white-haired man standing next to him. What amazed Rachel most were the odd clothes. Erik wore a green pair of leg coverings that went down only to his knees, and a white shirt.

"Who are they?" Erik was asking Timothy.

"Recognize the particularly stoned-faced lady on the far side?" Timothy asked.

Rachel felt an unexpected sensation of warmth and

excitement run through her as Erik's eyes locked directly on hers. "That's her—that's Rachel."

"These are her people. In a sense, they have done what you have, brought themselves out of time. Only they did it with oleander powder, a hallucinogen, which has the side effect of freeing the body from the mortal coil."

"Mortal coil? You mean it kills you?"

"Not permanently. Just takes the soul away from the body for a time. Many cultures, like this one, many religions, like your own world's Buddhism, have evolved based on the notion that freeing the mind and soul is possible.

"But the oleander powder's effect on their consciousness isn't strong enough to bring them completely out of their own minds. They're only partially experiencing this reality, while their minds remain anchored in their own. Essentially, they are trapped between realities. When you and I are speaking to each other, they will be completely unaware of it."

What? Rachel thought. But she could hear them. And it somewhat irritated her that they were having their own private conversation as if the others weren't here at all.

"You do realize, don't you," Timothy said, "that most of what you perceive as your reality is merely your mind's rough interpretation of the world around you, translated into the crude sphere of perception your five senses allow. Most mortal minds are doing little more than sleepwalking through reality. There are very few exceptions, thankfully. If a mortal mind were half as capable of experiencing actual reality as it was conjuring up its own, the mind would be a very powerful, very dangerous, tool indeed.

"Great being of time!" came Temara's voice. "You grace us with your presence."

"Now watch," Timothy said to Erik, "when we speak directly to them, it will be our thoughts they'll hear flowing directly into their minds. This will allow them to understand us without having their mind bothered by the cumbersome problem of language translation. They'll understand us instinctively."

Timothy cleared his throat and spoke in a much deeper, booming voice than he'd used to address Erik, "Ah, yes! Indeed! It is I! What mere mortal dares call me into being on this most powerful of nights?"

Erik cast the man a sideways glance. "Are you serious?"

"I have an image to maintain, the proper fear to command. I'm the great time being and all."

"Your words speak the truth, great time being, for tonight is indeed a night of great power. The goddess is smiling, for you have agreed to come to us this evening."

"What is she talking about?" Erik asked.

"I don't know. Just go along with her. She's so sure of herself. I'd hate to disappoint her."

"We call to you, we beseech you, we have just one request of you."

Rachel noticed that Temara was indeed proceeding as though she had no knowledge at all of Erik and Timothy's private conversation.

So why was Rachel aware of it? She wanted nothing more than to tell them she could understand their words, but the drug's hold on her was too powerful. The enchanting feeling of being trapped in the blanket of time was beginning to feel suffocating. Something about it felt unnatural. What the old man said made sense. The drug—whatever the women had drunk—trapped her in the moment. To speak to Timothy and Erik, what Rachel needed was to free herself from time, not be trapped in a sliver of it.

Rachel felt that a great war was being waged inside her. She found herself again wrestling with thoughts that maybe all the beliefs of her ancestors and the ways of the Priestesses weren't entirely correct. Here was Erik and Timothy, two men she had know before in a completely different context, standing before her Priestess. The scene was anything but what she would have expected. Temara was as serious, as somber as Rachel had ever seen her. And Timothy was the exact opposite.

It reminded Rachel of the way the old man had teased her that first afternoon she'd met him at the brook more than ten years ago.

Ten years ago? Temara had said that the last time she felt the presence of the goddess was ten years ago.

It was possible that was the same day Timothy had first appeared. She was certain he was not sent by any deity, and certain he wasn't a god himself. He was just a foolish old man who liked to toy with people by appearing like an apparition in water and in fire. That did seem like quite powerful magic, to appear at will out of the elemental earth, but that didn't make Timothy a god.

Rachel remembered the first time she and Claire met

him like it was yesterday, when the silvery haired old man had jumped in the brook after her, saying he was going to fish her out.

"Silly, the magic doesn't work that way!" she said.

"It doesn't?" Timothy said, feigning amazement and slicking his wet white hair back over his forehead. "Why didn't you tell me that before I jumped in the water and got myself all wet! I could have drowned! Drowned, I tell you!"

Rachel remembered thinking how funny he was and that there was no way he could drown in two feet of water.

"I tried to tell you before. You jumped in anyway. Besides, we're not fish," Claire said.

"You're not? Would it have hurt to tell me that too? But what else could you be? You live in the stream, after all. Here I thought I was talking to fish this whole time!"

"We're just girls, silly!" Rachel added. "We don't live in the water. You're just looking at us through it. We can just see each other's reflection, that's all."

"How old are you two? You're smart for your age," the old man said.

It made her feel good, and she liked Timothy immediately.

Rachel never expected to see Timothy toying with Temara the same way. Especially since Temara didn't even realize this was all some sort of game to the old man. She didn't realize he was no more a great time being than Rachel was a fish.

"Great time being," Temara intoned, "we have summoned you here to ask just one question of you."

"Ah, yes! Indeed!" Timothy thundered. "The great time

being is all-knowing. But beware! The knowledge of the remembered and the yet unremembered time can be dangerous and deadly. So ask your question; but fear the answer."

"Great time being," Temara called, "we seek to rid ourselves of the burdens of flesh and walk in the higher and as yet unremembered realm of existence."

"Ah, yes! Indeed!" he boomed once again. Then he turned to Erik and said, for Erik's ears alone. "Then lay off the drugs."

Rachel couldn't help herself. She giggled, which caught Erik's attention. He gave her a small smile. Embarrassed, Rachel was glad that none of the women seemed to notice any of it.

Timothy thundered once more, "Your desire has been shared by mortals throughout the endless ages of all recorded and unrecorded time! But alas! But one mortal soul has been able to accomplish such a great feat. In my omnipotence, I have anticipated your question and have brought this being of whom I speak with me to provide the answer!" Then, as a quiet aside to Erik, "Say something profound, Kherik."

"Like what?"

"Come on now! You're the only mortal being who's ever freed himself from the mortal coil and you can't think of anything to say? Just start with, 'Ah! yes! Indeed!' I find that usually works to get me started."

Erik gave Timothy a lopsided smirk, then cleared his throat, "Ah, yes!" he said, but couldn't bring himself to say, 'indeed.' It just seemed to melodramatic. "I say unto thee, noble warriors, thou australopithecine cave dwellers, thou shalt perform the ancient ritual of *mekazikazika!* Thou must perform *mekazikazika* for precisely one twenty-fourth of every day! Then, and only then, a worthy soul shall you be!"

No longer irritated that they were ignoring her, Rachel found herself thoroughly amused by Erik. She remembered Erik telling her that *mekazikazika* was what he did for one hour every day. And Erik had just said that his foolish exercise would unlock the secrets of the universe.

It reminded Rachel of nothing more than how she and Claire used to play make-believe as children, pretending they were great Priestesses and goddesses themselves, and that they controlled the way the sun merged with the earth, the way the seasons turned and the wind blew.

The closest they had ever come to having any real power was when she and Claire had been able to control the magic of the brook for a mere instant. They had transported themselves to the other side. The first time, they weren't even sure if they'd done anything at all. The world didn't seem any different. There had been a shimmer of white before their eyes, a feeling of nausea, but nothing else. The second time, the air on the other side was much colder. It was as though a gust of wind had blown all the warmth out of the air. But just as soon, the cold was gone and they were back in their own world.

It was as though every time they travelled between worlds, the magic was getting a stronger and stronger grip on them.

Rachel remembered a crisp day in late autumn. Cool but not cold. That was the only time they actually knew they had left their own world.

The sisters sat at the foot of the stream, assumed the posture of prayer, held hands and concentrated, clearing their minds of all thought, letting the world around them disappear from their minds. And then, it did.

Suddenly, inexplicably, they were sitting in snow, packed up to their waists, and lots more was falling from the cold gray sky. They could hardly see each other, it was swirling so fast. They were caught in a blizzard. It was bitterly cold and they were dressed lightly.

Terrified, the girls jumped to their feet instantly. Before, their own world had simply snapped back into existence mere seconds after they'd left. This time, that wasn't happening.

"Rachel, why aren't we home yet? We don't know how to get back!" Claire was frantic.

The wind was biting. There was no hope of achieving the calm meditative mind set that brought them here in their frightened, frantic state.

"We could freeze to death out here!"

The minutes they spent exposed to the powerful winter storm seemed like hours. Those were the longest moments of Rachel's life.

Finally, when their own world did snap back around them, they were shivering, and huddled up against each other together trying to warm up. Their cheeks were red and windburned, and clumps of heavy, wet snow clung to their light jackets and sandals.

They agreed they'd never tempt the magic like that again.

But now, today, everything was different. Claire was dead, and Timothy and Erik had given Rachel a reason to want to use the magic again.

She didn't know if she could summon it without Claire, or even if it could be done at all down here in the sacred caves, so far from the brook.

There must be some magic in the caves. How else could Timothy and Erik be here?

"Alas! Our time with you is limited," Timothy's thunderous voice boomed out again. "What did you call them, Erik? That was nice."

Erik smiled, "Australopithecine. Even better, how about .... Australopithecus afarensis."

"Ah, I like that," Timothy said to Erik.

Rachel willed herself to fight the drugs. She tried to cry out, "I can understand you!" But try as she might, no words escaped her lips.

Timothy bellowed, "Alas! We must make our departure! The great spirit Kherik will leave you with our final benediction!"

"I will?" Erik asked.

"Please do," Timothy said.

"Ah, yes! I bless thee now, noble warriors!" Erik cried out. "And wish thee Godspeed. Farewell unto thee, thou brave Australopithecus afarensis cave dwellers!" Erik cried.

Rachel wanted nothing more than to go with them, back to Erik's world or into the yet unremembered time, wherever it was they would be going.

"I can understand you!" Rachel cried out, at last. But she feared it was too late, because by the time the words left her lips, Erik and Timothy had already disappeared.

At the moment the time beings vanished from the flames, to the rest of the women in the room, it appeared as though Rachel had disappeared with them.

Temara smiled with satisfaction.

C H A P T E R

10

"QUITE A SHOW YOU PUT on for those people,"
Erik said to Timothy.

"Can't wait to hear the audience reviews,"
Timothy said. "I've no doubt they will be favorable. But,
right now, it's what *you've* done that we need to discuss."

"Me?"

"Yes. Do you have any idea where you are?" Timothy asked.

Erik had no idea. The vision of the cave had dissolved
before their eyes, and the white mist had gathered back in
all around them. But slowly, the opacity was thinning in
patches. A gnarled tree trunk was the first thing to appear.
Limbs grew out, jutting in every possible direction—and

some bent in ways that Erik wouldn't have thought possible. Gravel appeared at the base of its broad, ancient trunk. Then large rocks showed up in the gravel. Before his eyes, green moss grew on top of the rocks. Yet the shapes all appeared blurry behind a thin, translucent fog.

"It seems I'm standing in a bonsai garden," Erik said.

"You are outside of time," Timothy corrected.

"Oh, of course. Silly me. That clears it up," Erik said.

His feet suddenly felt very cold. He looked down. Not cold—wet. Of course they were. He was standing in a small stream running through the gravel. With a hop, he set foot back on dry ground.

Timothy paced slowly over to one of the mossy rocks and took a seat. "You have opened up your third eye and used it to travel along the seams in the fabric of time," the old man said. "I warned you what would happen if you didn't behave yourself."

"You gave me a riddle. Something about the unremembered time."

"Do you have any idea what it must have been like for little old me?" Timothy asked. "Here I am, peacefully minding my own business, tending my garden, when suddenly you just appear out of nowhere. Poof. Do you have any idea what that must have been like?"

Just as limbs continued growing spontaneously from the gnarled tree, the next thing to materialize out of the mist, was Rachel.

"It was *exactly* like that," Timothy said.

A look of wild-eyed excitement came over a speechless

Rachel. She walked toward the tree and gazed up into its spiderweb of outstretched arms. "Amazing. We could never grow anything like this is our world."

Just beside Rachel, a small, unassuming wooden meditation bench came into being. Without a second thought, Rachel walked over and sat down, crossing her hands in her lap, keeping a perfectly straight posture. She certainly seemed to fit right in.

"Timothy," she said. "You certainly had an interesting way of dealing with Temara."

"I'm glad you thought so," Timothy said. "See, Erik, I told you she'd approve."

"I didn't necessarily say I approve," Rachel resented having words put into her mouth, to say nothing of how Timothy addressed his comment to Erik, as if she wasn't sitting right there. "It actually seemed somewhat condescending," Rachel said.

Timothy brushed away the comment with a wave of his hand, "Semantics."

Rachel flashed Timothy a sour look then turned quickly to Erik, as if telling the old man she had more important matters to deal with.

"Erik, there's something I've been meaning to ask you," Rachel said. "Why are you dressed like that?" Rachel asked.

"Like this? These are my running clothes. I happened to be on a nice peaceful jog before I ended up here."

She reached out and felt the fabric between her thumb and forefinger. "Oh!" she exclaimed. "They're slimy! What in the world are they made out of?"

"Decomposed, liquefied and re-coagulated animal remains," Timothy chimed in.

Rachel could only stare at him.

"Polyester," Erik clarified. "And Timothy's colorful description is actually just about right."

"Well, they suit you, I guess," Rachel hesitated.

Erik wasn't sure how to take that. "Thanks," he said. "You seem to fit in quite well yourself." He indicated her posture on the meditation bench. "You look like you've been here before."

It occurred to Erik that maybe she had. She told him she'd known Timothy since she was a child. "Have you? Been here before?"

"No. You?" she asked.

"No. And speaking of which, Timothy, I'd still like to know exactly where here is."

Timothy cleared his throat. "If you two are done catching up, I was just about to explain exactly that.

"This," Timothy said with a sweeping gesture, taking in everything around them, "is my garden."

"A bonsai garden?"

"A garden of time," he said. "Just like a bonsai garden, it is only as much or as little as its caretaker. That's me, of course."

Erik and Rachel both stared at him with blank expressions.

Timothy cleared his throat. "Let's begin with the basics. Wormholes," he said flatly.

"Wormholes?"

"Yes, Kherik, you of all people should understand

wormholes."

"Why do you keep calling me Kherik?"

"Egads, boy! Didn't you even bother to read your parents' book? How do you think the Maya and Ancient Egyptians managed their global trade-route? Do you think they used boats? Flew airplanes? No, no, no. They were much too advanced for that."

His parents' book had gone so far to draw the conclusion that the many linguistic similarities between Mayan and Egyptian languages could not have developed independently of each other. Moreover, both cultures had very similar technologies and many of their respective pyramids seemed to have a twin halfway across the world. All of this pointed to the existence of contact between the Mayan and Egyptian civilizations, the book concluded. In fact, his parents postulated the existence of a global trade route that existed for nearly a thousand years.

"But of course you have no idea what I'm talking about," Timothy continued. "Perfect example of that cultural amnesia kicking in again. It's what Rachel's people would call the unremembered time."

"Are you suggesting the Mayans and Egyptians travelled through wormholes?" Erik asked.

"Across the seams of time, yes. Now imagine, if you can, a wormhole that not only connects two points in the same time and on the same Earth, but a wormhole that is neither bound to space, time, or even a single reality. Imagine that, and you'll be one step closer to understanding the true nature of the multiverse and the chronosverse. Now pay attention."

There was an earnestness about the old man that had quickly replaced his carefree demeanor in the caves. Rachel remembered seeing him like this once before, and it made her uneasy then, as it did now.

"Your world, Kherik, and yours, Rachel, occupy the same space and the same time, but both vibrate on a different frequency. Your universes are more than parallel. Together, they comprise a binary system. They are two sides of the same coin. Your two realities were once one in the distant past. With a mere toss of a cosmic coin, the fate of your two worlds could have been flipped."

Mind-boggling, Erik thought, but he didn't have much time to dwell on it, as Timothy continued right along.

"Erik, this is your universe," the old man said, and a thin ring of blue light appeared in his hand, hovering in the air just above his palm. It rotated and spun freely in three-dimensional space.

"Rachel's universe." This time a ring of red light appeared. It twisted itself around the first one.

"Do you see how the rings of light seem to be just floating in empty space? The space inside each circle of light is not empty at all. In fact, what looks like just empty space is actually your known universes. The red ring of light binds Rachel's universe together. The blue one binds yours together, Erik. Physicists on your world would call that ring a Higgs-Boson Field—the unseen force that binds your universe together. Your galaxy, your solar system, your planet, you, have all developed over the past fifteen-billion years in the space bound together by this simple energy, and every universe is bound together by its own field.

"Now, understanding that your universe exists within the energy field, you can grasp the principle of wormholes. Wormholes mean traveling not through the space of the universe, but on the perimeter of the field surrounding it, which is connected to every point in the chronosverse simultaneously—that is, the universe of time, or the garden of time, if you like."

"Which is *your* bonsai garden," Erik said.

"Precisely, yes! Now you're catching on!"

"Not exactly, no."

Timothy frowned.

"Wormholes exist independently of time, so travelling through them happens instantaneously. To travel from one universe to another, the same principle apples. You simply travel along the perimeter of one Higgs field to a point where it intersects with another field. Travel through space and time in this manner is an ability some religious leaders would attribute to opening up your third eye. But it makes no difference what you call it."

"Now," Timothy droned on, "your two universes are not the only ones in existence of course. There are a million billion more. Some stand alone, some are binary systems, some tertiary systems, but all are a part of the same whole. Watch."

One by one, additional rings began appearing, all perfect circles, all twisting around each other, all rotating and spiraling independently. Even as the number of intertwining rings increased, the overall size of the sphere that bound them together did not. It was as though all the new circles were simply finding room within the existing space.

Soon there were a dozen rings of light, and they were still appearing. Two dozen, and the number kept growing. Soon what Timothy held resembled a glowing ball of plasma, the individual circles barely distinguishable.

"Let's make this a little easier on the eyes," Timothy said. He wafted his other hand over the fiery ball, and the glowing light dimmed somewhat until the individual rings were visible once again. They coiled around each other like a ball of rubber bands.

"The universal continuum," Timothy said. "Now, imagine I can blow this up like a balloon."

Timothy raised the ball of rubber bands to his mouth, puffed out his cheeks and blew.

"What you're seeing now are a million Big Bangs, all resulting in the creation of new universes. What you're really witnessing is the creation of *reality*."

Miniature spheres began to expand from the surface of the main sphere like tumors on the surface. Soon there were a dozen miniature tumors, then two-dozen. The object Timothy now held was much larger than his hand.

"Like cells dividing," Erik said. "Each new sphere that splits off eventually itself splits again."

"Exactly," said Timothy. "Universal mitosis."

"Each individual circle represents one universe. Together, as a sphere, they represent the universal continuum. Now, I have a huge collection of spheres, called a hypersphere, which represents the multiversal continuum. Any guesses about what happens next?"

"The multiverse will undergo mitoses, too," said Rachel.

"Exactly. But don't be mistaken—this process does not go on infinitely. There is a limit. It will soon approach infinite mass."

Erik was glad to hear it. He and Rachel had to take a step back as the collection of spheres and hyperspheres was inflating at an incredible rate. The outermost spheres were just about to collide with the low-hanging branches of the bonsai tree.

"When infinite mass is achieved, what you'll witness is the creation of gravity."

Inexplicably, although Erik could clearly see that more new spheres were continuing to grow out from the edges of the massive shape, the overall size of the ballooning multiverse was now beginning to shrink.

"Now, watch what happens when it gets small enough."

The mass kept deflating, becoming ever more compact. When it was back to a size that fit once again into Timothy's palm, it stopped shrinking.

All the while, little flashes of light continued to play at the edges of the object. New spheres were still forming, though the overall object was no longer expanding nor contracting.

Until now, the object as a whole had always remained completely round. But Erik noticed that when it stopped shrinking, it flattened out, becoming an oval.

"What happened to it?" Erik asked.

"It began shrinking when it reached infinite mass. At that moment, you witnessed the creation of gravity, and it began to collapse under its own weight," Timothy explained. "It stopped shrinking when it achieved infinite density. That's when you saw the sphere flatten. What you witnessed at that moment was the creation of time.

"You see, infinite mass created gravity, which then caused infinite density. Infinite density created anti-gravity. The space inside became trapped between the two forces, gravity and anti-gravity. Under extremely strong gravity pushing in, and extremely strong anti-gravity pushing out, space can neither expand not contract, so it bends—flattens out. The bending of space is what we perceive as time."

"But if we saw the ball expanding and contracting," Rachel said, "that means something was happening to it, a change was occurring over time. From one second to the next, the system was changing. That means time must already have existed."

Her question took Erik by surprise. Was she actually following all of this? Back at the brook, she had been talking about things like her tribe, and magic. And she was the same woman who had taken part in a religious ritual performed by a Priestess. Erik had called her people Australopithecines. Even if they weren't the ancestors of modern humans, they certainly seemed to come from an iron-age-like society. So how could Rachel make sense out of concepts such as the space-time continuum ... let alone ponder the inconsistencies in Timothy's grand theory of everything?

"Excellent question, Rachel," Timothy said. "But we

were mere observers. Our time, yours and mine, already existed, that's why we were able to watch the mass expand and contract. We were on the outside looking in.

"What I am holding in my hand now is a closed space-time continuum, otherwise known as a Chronosverse. Literally, infinity in the palm of my hand.

"Even now, new universes and multiverses continue to form within it. Processes you would call 'big bangs' are occurring every second. But now, within a closed infinity continuum, those new regions of space-time don't have to exist simultaneously with each other. The system can continue expanding indefinitely, because time, when coupled with space, is infinite.

"Space had become finite, but the space within space continued to expand, so a solution was needed to avert the paradox. Time was the emergent property that arose to solve the problem."

"Emergent property?" Erik asked.

"An emergent property is any property that arises inexplicably. That means its existence is more than the sum of the parts that created it," Rachel said.

Erik's jaw dropped. "Thanks. How did you know that?"

Rachel shrugged modestly.

"That exactly right. Now, I'm holding in my hand my own little Chronosverse which continues to become more and more complex even as we speak. For millions of years, all the universes within will consist merely of empty space, and endless time .... and a little pinch of hydrogen. After another million years, some hydrogen will fuse into helium.

A million years after that, some helium might fuse into lithium, and on and on. In some universes, heavy elements may eventually form. In some of those universes, amino acids might come to exist, and in some of those universes, amino acids may even combine to form protein. One higher-level of complexity arising from the previous .... and on and on. Then, if all goes well within my Chronosverse, in several billion years, a small handful among the trillions of universes may become complex enough that the first emergent property—literally since the dawn of time—will emerge: life. Life is an emergent property of the universe."

"So what created life?" Rachel asked. "I mean, if time emerged to solve the paradox of finite space, what paradox did life emerge to resolve?"

"Now that," Timothy said, "is a true paradox. When a universe within a chronosverse attains a certain level of complexity, a sort of universal subconsciousness comes into being. In short, a universe becomes so complex that the sum of all its parts becomes, in essence, aware of itself as a whole. At that moment, life emerges as the universes' subconscious attempt to understand itself.

"Now here's the paradox. After billions of years floating around in gloppy seas, single-celled life forms evolve into fish, and fish into frogs and on and on, one level of complexity after another, until another emergent property arises: consciousness.

"Consciousness is what arises when life becomes so complex that it wants to understand itself. And that's the paradox. If consciousness is an emergent property of life, then how could life initially have come into being as an expression of the emergent property of the universe's subconscious? How could the universe have had a subconscious unless it had a consciousness, and how could it have had a consciousness if it wasn't first alive? And if it was already alive, why did it create you?"

"*Is* the Universe alive?" Rachel asked.

Timothy barked a laugh. "You tell me. You're the one who opened your third eye. Besides, we have no time to get into a philosophical debate," Timothy said.

"It would be better than listening to you drone on about things I can't even begin to fathom," Erik said.

"Drone on?" Timothy scoffed. "Thankfully, Kherik, not everyone here shares your limited intellect. Now Rachel," Timothy said, turning towards her,"please look again at this oblong sphere I hold in my hand. The inside represents the entire chronosverse. Our entire space-time continuum is contained within. Its outermost boundaries are like a cell wall—a semi-permeable membrane. You, Rachel, along with some others whose names we won't mention"—he threw a sidelong glance at Erik— "have developed the unique ability to pass through that membrane, and then re-enter at any point, in any universe, at any time."

"So, we're standing outside the chronosverse?" she asked.

"We are standing in a dimension that exists on the surface of time. Most life on Earth lives on the planet surface. Similarly, we are now standing on the surface of time. Not inside of it where we came from, but not really free of it either."

"And this is where you live—your species?"

"Our species is known as the Stakko Airos," Timothy said. It wasn't lost on Rachel that he completely dodged her question. "The best translation in your language is, well, your own Temara said it best: 'great time beings.'"

"Oh, please," Erik scoffed.

"Kherik, even *you* must be familiar with mythology. Do you know the story of Atlas?"

"The titan who held the world up on his shoulders?"

"Indeed!" Timothy said. "We are the Atlases of time. The only thing preventing time from collapsing in on itself is us."

To demonstrate, Timothy looked back down at the sphere in his palm. He reached in and with his thumb and forefinger, grabbed onto what looked like a single rubber band from inside the ball. As he pulled and pulled, the rubber stretched and stretched, until, finally, it snapped with the sound of a kernel of corn popping.

Then it sounded like a whole kettle started to pop. Loose ends started flopping out in every direction.

The popping grew louder, faster, until suddenly, the sphere simply vanished in a flash of white light.

"That's what we're desperately trying to prevent from happening to your space-time continuum," Timothy said. "The fabric of the cosmos is woven so tightly that too much tension on any one Higgs field will cause the entire Chronosverse to rip apart at its seams."

"What could possibly cause that to happen?" Erik asked.

"Why, my dear—you."

"Us?" Rachel cried.

"You and Erik both represent the awakening of a very unique and dangerous power. One which is an emergent property of consciousness itself, and unless stopped, will tear apart the very fabric of space-time."

CHAPTER

11

"I DO HOPE YOU'RE GOING TO explain that," Erik said.

"There's a lot more you'll need to understand before you can truly grasp what's at stake," Timothy replied. "But I'm afraid all my guests have not yet arrived at our little soiree. We are still one short. Why don't you two accompany me on a joyride through the cosmos. It'll be fun."

Erik was skeptical. For one thing, this wasn't exactly what he'd imagined lay outside the known world. He always imagined there was something more—call it a Heaven, Elysium, Shangri-La—by any other name, a bonsai garden in the middle of the mist didn't at all satisfy his preconceptions of what lie outside the known universe. There was something about the old man that didn't rub him the right way. He couldn't put his finger on exactly what.

"You are coming with us, Erik?" Timothy asked.

He had the strong impression it wasn't a question.

Despite himself, Erik said, "I wouldn't miss it."

"Good, then. But just one thing before we leave. I'll see if I can't do anything about making you more presentable. Rachel's right. You look ridiculous."

Erik had forgotten he was still wearing his running clothes, green shorts and a tee-shirt.

"I'd appreciate that," Erik said.

Timothy nodded, and suddenly things were vanishing from all around.

Much to Erik's dismay, it was his clothes that vanished first, then the bonsai tree, then the gravel, moss and rocks, then Rachel's bench.

The sound of water provided a segway between realities. Although the stream in the garden appeared to dry up, the soft bubbling remained and was now growing louder until it became a thunderous roar.

Erik found himself standing in a torrential downpour, hard rain driving into a muddy, blood-red Earth.

A wave of nausea overcame him when Erik realized where they were. It was the one place on Earth he wished he'd never see again. They were standing in the middle of a downpour in Madagascar.

One thing Erik forgot about the island were the hoards the malnourished chickens wandering aimlessly though the streets. They clucked noisily at all hours of the day, running chaotically from perch to perch, pecking at each other, fighting over dry spots that offered precious little shelter from the torrent. The chickens were as red and muddy as the roads they walked on, the rain fighting a losing battle to wash the splashing mud from their scrawny, feathered bodies.

The village appeared deserted except for the chickens. The afternoon daylight, heavily muted by the thick, dark storm clouds helped lend the impression of a deserted ghost town. No one was here to see three *Vazahas* simply appear out of thin air in the middle of the street.

A faint odor was barely noticeable over the scent of the rain. Erik couldn't place it, but it wasn't just the smell of wood smoke. Come to think of it, none of the chimney holes had any smoke billowing out of them—none, save one. It made sense that the villagers were all taking shelter from the rains under their tin roofs, but even so, the town seemed eerily deserted.

Erik didn't know if any of this was real or just another one of Timothy's illusions, like the bonsai garden. But things seemed more tangible here. From the strong odors, to the chickens and wild dogs brawling in the distance, to the touch of the gloppy, red mud plastering his legs.

At least I'm not standing here in the nude, Erik thought ruefully. As if sensing his thoughts, Timothy shouted over the rain, "The ponchos and galoshes were on back order, Erik, so I'm afraid you'll just have to make do."

Erik had to admit the heavy, durable jacket and trousers he wore were a big improvement. Not only that, the material was extremely comfortable. It was soft as cotton, but tough as suede. He stretched the back of the jacket over his head like a hood.

"It's made out of hemp," Timothy explained.

"Hemp? As in....the drug?"

"One of the most useful plants on Earth. Only a species with your limited capacity would perceive its hallucinogenic properties to be its most valuable asset."

"I've never worn anything like this."

"I wouldn't think so," Timothy said. "A plant! Outlaw a plant! I've never heard anything so absurd in my life."

Erik raised an eyebrow.

For her part, despite the rain, Rachel was in awe of the world around her. It was unlike anything she'd ever imagined. Structures the like of which she'd never seen lined the wide thoroughfare. The buildings bore a slight resemblance to the huts in her own village, but these were much grander, larger, and some were even made of wood and covered with sheets of a thin, shiny material that made a thunderous sound like the beating a drum with every drop of rain. Rachel couldn't imagine how anyone could stand to be inside of one these houses with all that noise.

Sloshing through the thoroughfare, Timothy was leading them to the nearest of the wooden homes, the only one with wisps of smoke climbing from its chimney.

"*Odeo! Akory!*" Timothy cried in the Malagasy language— "Hello! Welcome!"—as they approached the waist-high wooden gate guarding the entrance. Timothy's voice must have been lost in the cacophony of rain. When no one echoed back a reply, he reached over the gate to unhook the latch, and led them into the small muddy courtyard that lay beyond. Three similar-looking wooden structures flanked the courtyard.

It was a courtyard Erik had set foot in many times. This was where Ellia lived.

One of the three buildings was her family's home. The second housed another family, and the third served as a communal kitchen, which is where Erik went nearly every day while waiting out the last rainy season.

He didn't want to know what was beyond that door. Would Ellia be with yet another *vazaha* this season?

The Malagasy saying was, "The rain drowns out all work and the sounds of all lovemaking."

"*Akory!*" Timothy shouted again and opened the wooden door.

Erik stepped in front of Rachel so she wouldn't see what he feared they'd find inside.

When Ellia's eyes flicked open, she saw three silhouettes emerge from the glare as two men and a woman stepped into her pitch black chamber.

Alone in the dark, windowless room, she sat with crossed legs and palms upturned on her knees within a circle of burning candles, opening her eyes immediately when the muted sunlight and rain came pouring in.

As her visitors stepped further into the room, she could see now that it was Timothy who had thrown open the door. Ellia raised her lips into an upturned smile.

The last time she had seen the old man who now stood huddled in her doorway, he had made her a promise, and he had finally come back to make good.

Three months ago, crouched down on the rocks by the stream, busying herself with the menial, but necessary tasks of day-to-day life, Ellia's mind was far away from the clothes she was stone washing on the rocks.

Her body ached everywhere. Her face was swollen, her eyes black and blue, and she didn't even know what caused the sharp, stabbing pain in her side every time she stood up or sat down.

She had endured the last few weeks with an iron will, but was just about at her breaking point. The catcalls of *pamosavy* were nothing compared to everything that happened since Erik left her.

She heard someone coming up on her from behind. Ellia's mind snapped to attention. She stopped what she was doing and palmed the stone she used for washing. She darted to her feet so quickly the sharp stab of pain in her side was almost unbearable.

This was the last man she expected to see.

"Hello, *mon coeur*," the silver haired man said.

"What do you want?" she asked.

"My, my," Timothy said. "What has happened here?"

Timothy waved his hand softly through the air in front of her face and, instantly, the bruises were gone. He made the same gesture over the rest of her body and everywhere, her excruciating pain simply disappeared.

"Now perhaps you can help me with something," Timothy

said, reaching out to caress the side of her face. "I'm looking for someone I think you know. His name is Erik Nichim."

Eillia spat. "He is the one that did this to me!"

"Erik did this to you?"

"It's his fault. He slept with me. He abandoned me. He made those men do this to me. He turned me into *pamosavy!*"

"Erik Nichim did not turn you into *pamosavy*," the old man said.

"You don't know anything," she hissed at him. "I am *pamosavy* because of him! That is why all the men do this to me!"

"You are not *pamosavy* just because men think you are," Timothy said.

"No, if I *was pamosavy*, they would all be my slaves. I would kill them all with the lightning of the sky!"

"Well, which is it?" Timothy said, "Would you kill them or make them your slaves?"

"Maybe I'll kill you!" Ellia said, raising her fist overhead that still clutched the stone.

Timothy laughed. "I wouldn't put it past you. But how about this," he offered, gently taking hold of her wrist with one hand and uncoiling her fingers from the stone. "In exchange for my life, I will make you a promise. You see, you and I both want the same thing. We both want to find Erik Nichim. Believe me when I tell you that Erik Nichim does not have the power to make you into a *pamosavy*. But I do. He began your transformation, but abandoned you here, leaving you defenseless, without any power, unable to defend yourself. I'll finish what Erik began. I'll give you the power of *pamosavy*. I'll even deliver Erik to you. You may do with him as you wish. Kill him or enslave him. It will be your choice."

"Tell me what you want me to do," Ellia said, a smile creeping onto her lips.

"You've done enough for now," Timothy said. "All your pain and suffering, Ellia, has not been without purpose. It has made you strong. There is something else you can do for me, but first I have to find Erik Nichim."

"Take me with you."

"Not yet. There is work for you to do here. You must hone your new powers. Learn to control them, so you can help me in all that is to come."

That was the last time Ellia had seen the old man. Although the rainy season had ended around the time Erik had left Madagascar, when the old man left her there by the banks of the stream, the downpours suddenly began all over again.

That's when Ellia felt the change in her body. The old man, the time being, was not lying about the powers he promised to give her. She could feel them swelling inside.

The thunderstorms and midnight black skies came with them. When the lightning chased everyone indoors, Ellia relished the opportunity to taste her new power.

She imagined how the water of the heavy downpours would cleanse her soul after the acts she was about to perform, in the same way those acts would cleanse the whole village.

STANDING IN THE DOORWAY OF the dark kitchen, where Ellia now sat in a ring of candles, the old man had finally come back to her. This was her reward for all the hard work she'd done using the power he gave her.

"Mon coeur!" She leapt to her feet and fell into the old man's arms. Then, out of the corner of her eye, she noticed that Timothy was not alone. Erik was here too, with a female *vazaha* at his side.

She had no idea who the woman was, but Erik, his was a face she had dreamt so many times of seeing again.

It seemed the old man intended to fulfill all his promises today.

"You kept your promise!" Ellia shouted with joy when her eyes landed on Erik as she embraced Timothy.

Is she talking to me? Erik thought as a wave of apprehension came over him. *What promise did I make?*

"Of course I did, my dear," Timothy said. "Did you doubt me?"

It gave Erik pause to watch Timothy run his bony finger in a tender, affectionate caress down Ellia's cheek. So there was a connection between them. But how was that possible?

"You have to learn patience, my dear," Timothy cooed. "I gave you my word. This time, I'm taking you with me."

C H A P T E R

12

E RIK NOTICED GOOSE BUMPS ON RACHEL'S arms as a cold wind swept across the vast savannah, bending the grass that was almost knee-high in places. A seemingly endless plain of grasslands swept out so far and so flat that Erik thought he could view the curvature of the earth.

As far as the eye could see, moss-encrusted boulders of all shapes and sizes pockmarked the savannah. They were as dark as volcanic rock, but their origin was inexplicable. No volcanic activity appeared to have troubled this flat, alien world for countless eons.

The landscape had formed in front of Erik's eyes after a white shroud erased Ellia's candle-lit kitchen. When the veil had cleared, yet another alien world spread across the landscape, and a twinge of nausea had overcome him. Passing from one universe to the next felt like a mild electric current passing through his entire body. Every muscle tingled, as the world disappeared and reappeared.

And he always felt a bit queasy afterwards.

Erik found one of the large boulders to lean against until the feeling passed. Rachel must have felt it, too, wrapping her arms around her stomach, leaning forward and supporting her backside against one of the megalithic stones.

Ellia, for her part, stood with arms crossed, watching keenly the way a predator does its pray. Although she had been naked in the kitchen, she was fully clothed now, the folds of a black dress snapping in the strong wind.

She stood sentinel just a short distance behind Timothy, who was pacing restlessly in front of them.

"In this life, we are merely visitors to the earthy realms," Timothy was saying.

Erik needed to force himself to concentrate. There was a feeling of disorientation and exhaustion that accompanied each journey. He imagined it must be how deep sea divers felt if they emerged from the depths of the dark underwater world too quickly. Deep-sea narcosis could be crippling, even fatal. Erik wondered if he was experiencing some sort of spatial- or chrono-narcosis.

Although the passage between worlds seemed instant to the travelers, he wondered how much Earth-time passed each time they jumped. Seconds? Hours? Days?

"When I say earthy realms," Timothy continued, "what

I refer to are the interior realms of the chronosverse—the dimensions and planes of existence suitable for the evolution of life and consciousness. Each plane vibrates at a different frequency, some more strongly than others. The plane of existence that surrounds us here has one of the highest vibrations."

Rachel and Erik could in fact both feel a vibration resonating throughout the land beneath their feet. If he were to lay down, Erik imagined, it would feel quite pleasant, like a full-body massage. It was peaceful here, similar to the sense of tranquility he felt back home on the river. The land itself seemed to be sharing every breath he took.

"On each realm, in each multiverse," Timothy continued, "in every dimension that now nurtures advanced beings, there came a fork in the road of evolution—a point at which life became significantly complex in its chemistry and design that an emergent quality spontaneously and inexplicably developed. Consciousness. The first self aware life forms evolved sporadically, but soon they were popping up everywhere, and soon there with more civilizations in the chronosverse than stars in a single universe. And now here we are, an infinite infinity of immeasurable time later, and it's these realms of consciousness that make up the very core of the chronosverse, the deep interior of existence. What's more, all the realms of existence on which conscious beings evolved are inter-connected. The universes that have evolved consciousness are all interwoven. For example, your world, Erik, is coiled around Rachel's world. Her reality co-exists with yours at precisely the same moment in time, but on a different dimensional plane.

"The brook where you and Rachel first met is part of a nexus where the two Higgs fields from your respective universes meet. Wherever two fields conjoin, a gravity well manifests itself. Most can be seen with the naked eye. There's usually some physical manifestation of these regions, which flow like rivers through space-time. Many times, actual rivers and lakes form. Water naturally flows to areas of the strongest gravity.

"The place we are standing in right now, on Earth, is at the center of Stonehenge. On this plane, life has never evolved. Nevertheless, these volcanic rocks, haphazardly strewn about by the powers that be, mark the spot.

"For millions of your years, millions of realms have existed in harmony and balance and it has been the role of the Stakko Airos to maintain that balance."

"You're claiming you're supreme beings?" Rachel asked.

"Supreme?" Timothy chucked. "We make no claims of supremacy, no. Although in our travels we have come across no civilizations, no beings, more evolved than we are."

"How long have you—"

"Once space-time continuum is closed, and infinity created, time has no beginning, and no end," Timothy said. "We have been the guardians of your chronosverse for longer still. The origin of our own consciousness pre-dates yours by an infinite number of re-incarnations of your universe. We have existed so long, in fact, that we have lived to see the day we always feared was coming. Recently, the tearing of the seams of time, which we have for so long been trying to prevent, has finally begun."

"Tears in the seams of time?" Erik asked

"Yes, it is being shredded apart by you and those like you. For millennia, sentient beings have been attempting to expand their knowledge of the possibilities of consciousness, to break into the other realms of existence. For millennia, we have successfully guarded the realms against breaches by mortal beings.

"The power you and Rachel have unlocked allows both of you to travel along the seams of time, from one plane of existence to another. But each time a vein of time is tapped in this way, used as a conduit, more and more force is exerted on it. The fabric of space time becomes stretched and thin, like pulling on a rubber band. You are the first two humans to have breached the realms since the distant past. Last time this occurred, we barely managed to contain the power before it tore the universe to shreds. One or two wayfarers does not pose a significant threat, but even now, there are places within the universe where the secret is as widespread as the knowledge of fire. Already the lines are being drawn. There are those who would see the fabric of space-time ripped to shreds so that they can expand their own personal horizons of consciousness. For millennia, the gates between the planes have remained sealed. And this is how it must remain. This unearthly life was never meant for mortals. I ask you, is the evolution of a single species worth tearing the universe to shreds?"

"Well," Erik scoffed, "when you put it that way."

"Again with the insolence! You impudent being!" Timothy cried.

"Where did this power come from?" Rachel asked, trying to diffuse the tension. "How is it that I managed to bring myself ... out of time?"

"A mistake," Timothy said. "A power which never should have been re-awakened."

"But, *how*, Timothy?"

"The important question is how to reverse the process. I fear a chain of events has been set into motion that cannot be averted. On ancient Earth, when amino acids in the primordial soup combined to form the first proteins, the inescapable result, eventually, was you. Destructive, warlike, aggressive."

"You're describing only the darkest qualities of humanity," Erik said.

"I am describing the most pervasive qualities of humanity. That which you call civilization proves that consciousness was the universe's greatest mistake. It was a blunder for the universe to allow consciousness ever to evolve."

Rachel said, "Timothy, you said that consciousness is an emergent property of life. So if this power Erik and I have is simply an emergent property of consciousness, it's just evolution. One level of complexity arising from the last. It all sounds very natural. How can that destroy the universe?"

"From the moment life developed consciousness, it began to believe it could choose its own destiny," Timothy said. "But life is merely one thread in the vast tapestry of the universe. What you fail to realize is there are consequences to your actions that will effect things far beyond your realm of comprehension. Nothing better illuminates the inability of life to fully comprehend the consequences of its actions than the maudlin behavior the multiple human species have demonstrated throughout their dismally unsuccessful histories."

"Unsuccessful?" Erik said. "Look at everything civilization has accomplished over the millennia."

"Look at it all indeed," Timothy said. "Every civilization you've ever managed to create has always collapsed. Humanity has been a miserable failure at everything it's ever attempted. Your species has a lot of anger, you know. Or is it frustration at the universe? Are you simply tired of failing at everything? Whatever it is, the only thing you've ever been any good at is destroying things. And this time it appears as though you just may succeed. You've been destroying your own civilizations for thousands of years. But like a nasty infection, you just keep coming back. But not this time. You've been on the verge of destroying the Earth's entire ecosystem for the past century. And with this new power you've evolved, Erik, humanity might actually destroy the entire universe along with its own planet."

"I don't know what it's like on Erik's world, but my people are peaceful."

"They may be now. They weren't always," Timothy said.

"That's the point. We *evolved.* This ability to travel outside of time is evolving, too. Give us time," Rachel said.

Erik, too, found himself considering alternate viewpoints to Timothy's explanation. He couldn't necessarily defend humanity against Timothy's accusations. Much of it was the harsh truth. But hearing the old man attack his entire species made him feel defensive—no, there was a better word for it than that.

Erik thought he could see a silver lining. Was his species truly embarking together down a new evolutionary path? Was it humanity's destiny to develop into a life form that could travel freely throughout reality? Erik imagined beings of pure thought, pure consciousness, free from their corporal form, free from suffering, from death.

Was that truly human evolution's next step? If it were true, it could bring hope to millions of people on Earth who saw their lives as meaningless. The knowledge that humanity was destined for something greater, and knowing what that might be, could unite the species in the promise of hope for the future. Realizing that all of humanity was evolving together, towards enlightenment, at one with the cosmos, could unite humanity as never before, end war, poverty, greed.

Could it even provide the spark necessary in the 11th hour to avert the environmental collapse humanity was causing on Earth? Timothy was right about civilization destroying the planet. But there was still hope, still time.

"There is no more time," Timothy said. "Mortals will always be malcontents. This power will not change your nature. Your race would see it as a *supernatural* ability, and it would merely degenerate into a religion with time. The more power humans have, the more corrupt and greedy they become. Which is why we must prevent this ability from taking seed."

"But what gives you the right to alter the natural course of human evolution?" Erik asked, his anger growing.

Now he knew what he was feeling in reaction to Timothy's rant against humanity, his assertion that the race as a whole was not worth saving. Erik was feeling patriotic. Not for a country or a king, but patriotism for his species. Taking a step away from the boulder he was leaning against, he assumed a more assertive posture. "You have no right to choose our destiny for us, and I can't imagine it's within your power."

Behind Timothy, Ellia offered the first sign she'd been paying attention to any of this. She sensed the tension, and glowered at him with her cold blue eyes.

Erik's temper was still rising.

The witch-woman leaned in slightly, her hands on her hips, her sharply angled jaw giving her the appearance of a vulture poised to strike.

"Our powers far exceed anything your human mind can comprehend," Timothy said.

Rachel felt the situation escalating out of control. Ellia had the look of a well-disciplined sentinel standing guard. She had come alive now that Erik was cornering Timothy. Rachel had learned enough from the warriors of her tribe to know you never wanted to make a wild animal feel threatened.

But when Timothy raised his hand, Ellia obediently backed off. "Let's keep this civil," Timothy said. "You simply don't understand the true enormity of the situation. You have both proven your ability to arrive here of your own volition. Which means you can pass the power along to others of your species. That makes you both very dangerous. I have come to ask for your help in the battle against those who would destroy the barriers between the realms, tear forever the fabric of space-time."

"What about her?" Erik asked, pointing to Ellia. "What's her part in all of this?"

"I gave her what she always wanted. Freedom. In exchange, she is helping to maintain the continuity of space-time."

"You played to her desire to leave Madagascar. But how is bringing her out of time helping?"

"You may yet find out, Kherik," Timothy intoned.

Erik didn't understand all of it, but the furrowed look on Rachel's brow told him her mind was locking pieces in place he was probably only vaguely aware were laid out before them. He was dying to know what was going on in her mind. But she was keeping her peace. She struck him as someone who wouldn't leap before looking. Rational. Calm. Collected.

Even from what Erik was getting out of all of this, there were a few things about Timothy's story that didn't seem to add up.

"Timothy, I don't know how long you've truly been here or what the origins of your species are, but if the evolution of life occurred just as you described it all throughout the universe, it seems that your race must have once been very much like ours is now," Erik said. "Mortals. Existing on some earthly realm, as you put it."

It was Erik's comment that made the missing piece snap

into place for Rachel. She remembered the new perspective she had gained at the sacred caves. Claire's death had shown her there were some beliefs that were merely convenient to hold onto. Are the dead really become reborn? Rachel supposed no one would ever know—not really. Yet her people chose to believe that the goddess offered the gift of rebirth. Because it was comforting to believe that. It was convenient. But that didn't necessarily make it true.

"I believe sentient beings evolved in this universe for a reason," Rachel said. "I've always felt it at the grove. I feel it here in this place .... I feel connected to everything around me. Call it the chronosverse, the universe, the goddess. I feel that the universe is alive. It's alive within us. It knows I'm here. It simply must have known life was coming, and it wants life to evolve. I can't believe that following the path evolution would lead us down can only end in the annihilation of the universe. That surely must not be the inescapable result of evolution. As Erik said, your people must have evolved very much as ours are doing now, and despite that, the universe is still here. There's more to the story that you're not telling us."

"Impeccable logic, as always. Deducted by a being who holds free will in the highest regard. What charming arrogance. I'll simply have to make you understand."

When every nerve in Rachel's body began to tingle again, she knew they were being whisked onto yet another plane of existence.

C H A P T E R

13

OUT OF THE VASTNESS OF THE sweeping blue sky and the flat, endless plains, another alien world emerged. The grasslands beneath their feet transformed into a cavernous expanse of mist-enshrouded valleys nestled between enormous, snow-capped mountains.

Their aerial view of the breathtaking vista revealed one chasm directly below them that was enormously deep. It was a series of tiered glaciers.

On the highest tier, breaking through the swirling mist protruded tall, sharp spires, turrets and parapets adorning an immense palace. The central structure was covered by what looked like a single sheet of stained-glass, and eight vaulted passageways, like gangly arms, spiderwebed out from it. Flying buttresses supported the floating tunnels which spanned the length of the valley, terminating in the surrounding mountainsides.

A pair of stairways reached their long legs down the tiered glaciers, offering entrance to the palace from below. Erik couldn't imagine how many steps there might be. A thousand? Two thousand? It was mind-boggling.

Overlooking all of this, four visitors to this distant and miraculous realm found themselves standing on a sheet of ice, facing into a biting wind.

The prospect of traveling through the vastness of the cosmos and all its incumbent dimensions at the snap of a finger made Erik feel a sinking sensation deep in his stomach. Either that, or it was the sheer drop off less than a foot from where they stood. From here, Erik saw no clear way to gain access to the structure below. Any invaders from this elevation, though possessing the high ground, would have found the stronghold completely impregnable.

Erik was aware of a soft rumble, like thunder, far off on the horizon. But the sky was azure blue. No storm clouds. No rain. No lightning. Where was the thunder coming from?

"Behold, the battlefield of evolution," Timothy announced. It was apparently neither the palace before them, nor the glacier beneath their feet that Timothy had brought them here to marvel at.

Timothy was pointing at a field of ice and snow far below the palace where the base of its gangly staircases terminated. There, on the frozen field that extended as far as the eye could see, two armies were clashed in battle.

Looking like miniature toy soldiers from this distance, Erik could discern that they were equipped with crude implements of warfare: metal shields and helms, axes and broadswords that made the battle all the more violent. The snowy field was dyed with ribbons of crimson that flowed like rivers in slow motion across the endless glaci-ated expanse. The size of the battling armies was dizzying, a dark mass of clashing bodies clumped together in two opposing front lines, extending from horizon to horizon. The line undulated like a wave, with peaks and troughs cresting between countless dead already lying still upon the crimson snow.

Erik noticed something strange. The bodies of the dead didn't lay still for long. They disappeared in a flash of blue light. Sparks flickered all up and down the front lines as bodies miraculously disappeared.

And both armies were in possession of a seemingly endless supply of reserves, hoards of men waiting en masse to make their way to the front line. The size of those hoards never seemed to shrink. In fact, it almost seemed to be growing.

"Each warrior possesses the power you have discovered. One army, that of the Queen of this plane of existence, are the savages whose victory in this war will spell the end of continuity to your space-time continuum. The other is an army that fights with us, defending the known universe from its own inhabitants who would destroy it."

As Timothy explained, Erik heard the rumble on the horizon growing steadily louder.

"This battle has been fought a hundred times over, as history continues to repeat itself. Our army has proven victorious in most of the campaigns, but not all. There are other battles on other planes, other warriors who have been locked in combat, like these armies, for millennia. There is no escape from the battlefield for them. As soon as they die, they are reborn to fight again."

A soft tremor shook the earth beneath Erik's feet. But no sooner than it begun, the tremor subsided, and the sound like thunder became softer and softer, until it had receded quietly back into the horizon.

"This is a war for the continuity of space-time. It has no end, and no beginning. Now that is has begun, it can never end. There can be no victory until the universe is either destroyed or the savages can be made to see reason. Thankfully, the battle for this realm is going in our favor. Amethyst Kate, the Queen, is beginning to see reason. I believe she will call for her troops to surrender soon enough."

Erik could only stare stone-faced at the horrors playing out below, trying to grasp the enormity of it all. He was jolted out of his thoughts when a sharp, stabbing pain erupted in his backside and spread quickly throughout his body. It was like every nerve ending caught fire.

He turned around sharply and found himself staring into cold, merciless eyes that shone out from a gruff, leathery mask of flesh.

"Don't move," the man growled.

The sharp object that had been digging into his back was now pointed at his throat. A dozen armored men flanked

Erik and his captor.

"So," one of them drawled, "at last the emissary of peace returns." He backhanded Timothy across the face with a hand equipped in metal armor, the talons protruding from each knuckle now red with blood.

Ellia erupted with a roar and struck out against her captor, but she was no match for the three additional men that surrounded her.

"The Queen will not be pleased that you have returned."

That was the last thing Erik remembered before a searing pain erupted on the back of his skull, and his world went black.

His senses returned just as jarringly. Erik found himself being dragged on his backside over mercilessly rough, cold ground, his hands shackled together above his head.

A blindingly bright sky looked down on him and stiff winds howled ferociously. His backside felt numb against ice.

Turning his head, he saw Rachel, Timothy and Ellia sharing his predicament. Each were bound in the same manner he was, being dragged by one of the burly, broad-shouldered soldiers.

Erik met Rachel's eyes, which offered him some sense of comfort, though he couldn't bear seeing her so helpless.

"That's enough," came a smooth female voice.

And their trek across the ice halted.

Erik slowly managed to flip over and rise to his feet, despite his muscles crying out with stiffness and pain.

"So, the Stakko Airos return. Oh, my apologies, the *great*

time being returns. And who have you brought with you this time? More slaves, I presume?"

A lithe, female figure approached, her head and face covered by a shaggy hood, an extension of the brown fur that ran the length of her lanky body.

"How very nice to see you again, m'lady," Timothy answered, "Excuse me, my *Amethyst*. I trust you've come to remove your brutes and offer me the appropriate benediction."

"My brutes are the appropriate benediction!" the figure glowered. "And I won't call them off until I know exactly why you've come among us again."

"My dear Amethyst, I have brought visitors from the lower realms to witness this most historic of occasions."

"And what history are we making here today? Or would un-making be the appropriate term?"

Timothy said confidently, "Today is the day your troops shall lay down their arms."

Thrusting that same sharp weapon into Timothy's back, his captor sent the old man falling to his knees.

The seemingly simple club inflicted much more pain than it should have been physically capable of.

"The emissary of peace indeed," growled the captor. "Come to demand the terms of our surrender. The insolence! You will show the appropriate respect to Amethyst Kate!"

The man struck Timothy another hard blow.

"Captain," the shadowy female said, "that will be enough."

She removed her hood to reveal smooth, pale flesh, feminine and untouched by neither sun nor the inhospitable climate. It was a far cry from the leathery flesh of the soldiers under her command.

Looking at the old man whose body was doubled over in agony, "What are your terms?" almost under her breath.

"TIMOTHY, I BEG YOU. END this," Amethyst Kate implored. "You can't know what it's like. The consequences of this war are unimaginable."

"Amethyst, not only can I imagine it, I told you myself what road you were leading your people down."

"You didn't tell me what kind of world would arise out of the chaos. There was no way we could possibly have foreseen these consequences."

Thunder rumbled again, and Erik thought it felt much stronger where they were now, deep inside the palace.

They stood in the center of a chamber so vast it made him dizzy. Eight walls formed an octagon out of the room, each solid stained glass and rising from a mirror-smooth black marble floor to an arched translucent ceiling at least twenty feet high, vaulting to at least double that height in the center of the chamber. The ceiling served as a brilliant skylight, its frosted glass evenly diffusing the daylight.

As the rumble of the earth became stronger, the stained glass walls began to vibrate, which passed into the dome overhead, causing an eerie shimmering of the light.

"Timequakes," Timothy said.

"Timequakes, indeed," Amethyst Kate said. "Are responsible for what's become of my world."

The quake subsided, almost reluctantly.

"On the contrary," said Timothy, "Timequakes are the

result of what you're doing to your world."

"I have no stomach for debate, Timothy. The bounds of reality are disintegrating all around us. The carnage of war, young men dying, starvation, pestilence, that's the only kind of warfare we have ever known. But we're living in a world where time has no meaning. Cause and effect is negated. After a timequake yesterday, a girl I had never seen before embraced me and said she was my daughter. The day before, my mother was still Queen. Every quake brings new variables, elements from other realities that have no place here. When I go to sleep each night, I have no idea if I will awaken in a reality where I am Queen of a proud, people, or a slave in the iron mines. Or whether my civilization that has endured for a thousand generations will ever have existed at all."

"Your world has become unanchored from its port," Timothy said. "It is adrift in a vast sea of parallel realities."

"These timequakes began the last time your people visited us, Timothy," Kate accused him.

"The last time we visited you," Timothy rebuked, "it was to deliver a warning. If your people continued to evolve their new-found abilities to travel outside the space-time continuum, your entire reality would suffer the consequences. The stubbornness of your people has caused the timequakes, not us. This is the path you yourselves have chosen."

"The last time you visited us," Amethyst corrected, "you threatened us with annihilation. You said my world was merely a grain of sand on an infinite shore, and told me a monsoon was coming."

Responding to her words, another rumble shook the walls.

"And your lofty palace is no more than a glorified sand castle!" Timothy proclaimed, "which will be razed by the tide of time which you have unleashed. Time is an unstoppable force that will hammer down these walls, your world, and unmake everything you've ever known. Unless you let me help you."

"Timothy, please, I beg you, if it is within your power...."

"There is nothing that is not within my humble power."

"Then stop this, Timothy. Restore time to its natural course ... and we will do whatever you wish."

"My dear Amethyst, all you had to do was ask."

"There is just one condition," Amethyst Kate intoned.

"I am not here to make bargains," Timothy said.

"Timothy, I find you to be a loathsome, manipulative being. And the Stako Airos are no friends of time."

"No friend of time? Amethyst, you wound me."

"My condition is merely this, Timothy: Once you leave this plane of existence, you never return."

"My dear Amethyst," Timothy said, "don't flatter yourself. Time may be endless, but I would never dream of squandering any more of it by ever returning here."

C H A P T E R

14

A MILLISECOND OF DARKNESS EXPERIENCED IN THE blink of an eye was all the time it took to change the world completely. The shelter of the vaulting palace hall was suddenly gone, and a cool wind blew once more across a vast savannah. These same grasslands, Timothy had told them, in another world—Erik's world—housed Stonehenge.

Erik had seen Stonehedge once. He'd even gone for a run in the English countryside that same day. He remembered it vividly.

It was hard for him to accept those gargantuan boulders weren't truly as permanent as the stones they were made of. The monument itself, the ancient human civilization they were a testament to, even the countryside on which the megalithic stones were assembled, it all existed in but one reality. And this time being, standing before them now, claimed to exist in all realties, everywhere—that he could travel across the vast sea of time in the blink of an eye, more effortlessly than humans sailing across the ocean. Did that make his existence more concrete than Stonehenge?

"Now you see what is truly at stake," Timothy said. "The outcome of this war will decide weather time is ripped apart at the seams, or if it is not too late to salvage something of your universe."

"You're not very well liked on that realm," Erik observed. "And on many others, I would suspect."

"Yes, well," Timothy brushed it off, "a hazard of my profession. Conscious beings—especially those like Kings and Queens who fancy themselves rulers and guardians of civilization—have the misguided impression they are in control. But no matter. It's something we're well prepared to deal it—it's a quality my own species sees quite often in our own offspring."

"Implying you see humanity like children?"

"They act like children—along with all the other species of lower consciousness. But no, they are most definitely not our children. And a good thing, too. We have much better things to do than prance around playing god. Now, we must not waste any more time. Despite our victory in Kate's reality, the seams of time are tearing in many other places. We must act quickly."

"Not so fast," Rachel said before Timothy could simply snap his fingers and they found themselves aimlessly displaced in some other random reality.

"That's the second time you've denied your species being gods. So, what *does* give you the right to interfere with the evolution of the universe?" Rachel asked. "In fact, another possibility seems to present itself. What if it's not the evolution of conscious beings that's causing the discontinuity of time, but your invasion of time? It could be your interference with the natural evolution of the universe is causing the very tearing of reality you're trying to stop."

Erik was deep in thought, "I agree. I'm not ready to subscribe to the version of events you would have us believe, Timothy."

"Impudent beings! It's your backwards beliefs in the self-righteousness of your own kind that's causing this. What gives *us* the right? What gives *you* the right to annihilate the universe simply so your own petty life form can evolve? You are a parasite on Earth. You are a bacterial infection in the universe. But it's no matter. The universe may very well have known you were coming to infect it, but we will be the ones who heal it. The power you both possess cannot be allowed to spread."

Timothy snapped his fingers.

Ellia suddenly emerged, as if walking out of the shadows themselves, grabbed Erik by the throat and, with incredible force, hurdled him twenty yards through the air, slamming his body into the nearest boulder.

Ellia crossed that distance in no more than a blur of light

and renewed her grip on his throat, preventing his body from falling to the ground after its violent impact with the rock. Pain rushed through the back of his skull.

"Many months I've waited for this opportunity. Since you left me there to rot in that world. I'm going to enjoy this, *Vazaha*."

Her iron grip was choking him. He watched in horror as she raised her other hand, and a ball of coiling blue lightning formed in her palm. Her bright eyes glowed with red fire.

The lighting shot out of her palm in a bolt that made the very air it touched sizzle. When the lightning tore into Erik, a searing pain erupted in his chest. He felt his heart beating faster, frantically, erratically.

Suddenly there was shouting all around. Erik heard Rachel's voice screaming out, and Timothy shouting at her, but Erik couldn't focus on anything beyond the pain.

The last thought that went through his mind before his body fell to the ground, was that it wouldn't be long before the electric charge Ellia sent surging through him would stop his heart.

SINCE ERIK ABANDONED HER IN Madagascar, trapping her in that world, Ellia endured more pain, agony and humiliation than any human should have to. Thanks to him, only a small part of her remained human; the other part had already begun its transformation into *pamosavy*.

When the men stoned and kicked her at the taxi station, Ellia used her anger to harden her resolve and endure it.

When the three men snuck up on her in the dark alley a

few days later, Ellia suffered their catcalls, fists to her face and boots to her stomach with indignity. The anger was her only defense. Her directed rage seemed to diminish the physical pain. Nothing could compare to the seething hatred she felt for the one man who had caused this to happen to her. It was all because of Erik.

Someday, she would have her revenge. She knew it. She would kill all of the men who had ever hurt her, every last one.

Soon Ellia reached her breaking point. As if sensing her great need, that's when the old man had come to her at the river and gave her the greatest gift she could have imagined.

Today, it was time to use it. As much as she desired to make Erik her slave, watch him suffer as she had, she didn't know how she could possibly control herself when killing him would give her such immediate, intense pleasure.

C H A P T E R

15

RACHEL SAW ELLIA TAKING LONG, SWIFT strides over the grassland, but knew Erik hadn't. Her lanky body seemed to separate from the long shadows cast by the boulders. Ellia's long legs and graceful gait made short work of the distance separating her from Erik and blind-sided him.

The sensation that welled up deep inside Rachel's gut as the witch woman grabbed Erik by the throat and slammed him into the boulder almost sent Rachel collapsing to the ground herself.

It was a powerful sensation, born out of horror watching what Ellia was doing to Erik, born out of indignation at being powerless to stop it, born out of the sheer power of the land Rachel felt coursing beneath her feet, what her people called the Veins of Earth.

Behind her, Rachel heard Timothy chuckling. "I have no control over what has been set into motion. We are merely the guardians of this place. The citizens themselves fight the battle. As I said, the lines are being drawn."

That tone of satisfaction, the joy in Timothy's malevolent chuckle made the power well up even stronger inside Rachel.

"No!" she shouted, and sprinted across the distance towards Erik, just as the lighting in Ellia's palm began to touch his chest.

Rachel threw herself at Ellia and the two women tumbled to the ground and Erik collapsed.

Rachel found herself at a crippling disadvantage, with Ellia pinning her down, holding her by the wrists and digging a knee into her pelvis.

The witch's eyes were aflame, and in that moment, Rachel felt sheer terror. What had she done? She was dealing with forces far beyond her comprehension. Then again, she had been doing that her entire life—she simply hadn't known it. The funny old man at the stream was anything but what he appeared, and probably older than she could imagine. Her clan's Priestesses, too, practiced a far darker magic than she had ever imagined possible. Nothing at all felt familiar, except maybe Erik, a man from the other side she'd only just met. Was he even still alive? Had she acted soon enough? The thought of Erik renewed the powerful sensation she felt deep in her gut.

Staring into the eyes of the witch hovering over her, the storm in her soul broke. Blue lightning arched from Rachel's own palms, slamming into Ellia and throwing her a dozen feet into the air.

Rachel came to her feet and ran towards Erik. She took him in her arms, and without thinking about it, started kissing his face and sobbing. "Erik, Erik! You have to get up. Can you stand?"

He was silent, his body motionless, but she felt a very weak pulse.

Rachel looked up and saw both Timothy and Ellia coming towards them, quickly. She didn't know what she'd done, but simply knew she still had access to that power deep inside her.

"Leave us alone!" she shouted at Timothy. "You're both witches!"

"Rachel, listen to me," Timothy said. "Your mind still remains largely unaware of the power you have managed to summon. Come with us, and we can teach you how to control it, use it to help us re-seal the gates of reality."

"Timothy, you terrify me more than whatever power I have." Rachel clenched her teeth, closed her eyes, and grabbed firmly onto Erik's body, his breathing very shallow. Tears streamed down her face.

No, she couldn't let her sadness and fear envelop her. She had used her emotion as a weapon before, to summon the lighting.

She concentrated, hard. She thought about Erik, about the brook, about her home, about how since her sister died, her world had come crashing down around her. She wanted nothing more than to return home, for everything to just be back the way it was before any of this began.

This isn't real, none of this is real. And it was with that thought that reality vanished in a frost of pure, white light.

WHEN THE WORLD REMADE ITSELF around her, at first Rachel wasn't sure they were anywhere at all. The effect of the world vanishing and remaking itself took place in a white haze of light, and that's exactly what this new world looked like: white. It looked much like the void where Timothy had grown his bonsai garden.

But then, slowly, her eyes started picking out soft details around her. Barely discernible behind a velvety fog, a line of pine trees stood not too far off.

She still cradled Erik in her arms, hanging on to life by a thread.

Then she heard something, softly, in the distance that she recognized. A song.

I've been here before, Rachel thought. She used to love that song as a girl.

"At my back I always hear
My chariot coming near...."

A young child's voice was singing. And suddenly Rachel knew exactly where they were. And they most definitely were not safe here.

There was only one time in her life she could remember ever seeing fog this thick. At the brook. The last time she and Claire had seen Timothy there.

The melody continued,
"...*And now before me lies*
The palace of eternities."

It was her. She was the one singing. And Claire! Claire would be here, too.

The thought of seeing her sister again sent a cold shiver down her spine. What she wouldn't give....

But Rachel also remembered that Timothy was with a dark woman that day—Ellia!—and they were pursuing a man and a woman, running through the forest.

It was her! Timothy and Ellia had been chasing her and Erik!

And that meant Erik was going to be alright! He would live... He would be running.

Knowing that he must live, that she had seen him alive, running away from Timothy and Ellia, gave Rachel hope.

A rustling sound came from behind them somewhere unseen, in a world masked by fog.

"Erik, please," she implored. "Please Erik." She placed her hand on his chest. An orange light began to glow between her fingertips, and then it flashed suddenly, making the mist all around them glow a bright crimson for a split second.

Erik's body stirred. Rachel started to cry with joy and bent her lips to Erik's forehead where she began trailing soft kisses down his face.

Through a numbing pain, Erik became slowly, vaguely aware of the gentle touch of soft lips on his cheek and as he opened his eyes, he thought that waking up had never before felt like such a pleasant dream.

"Where are we?" he asked.

Rachel sobbed. "We're not safe," she said, and helped him to his feet.

Behind her, Erik saw Ellia and Timothy emerge from the mist.

"Come on, I'm alright," Erik said, and, pulling Rachel by the arm, began running with her, hoping they could hide under the cover of the pine trees he saw.

The last thing he remembered was Ellia's stranglehold, a lot of shouting, and then waking up being kissed by Rachel.

She must have done it. Rachel must have saved them. Somehow whisked them away, out of time to come here.

But Timothy and Ellia had been able to follow. So they had to do it again, but this time, to somewhere Timothy and Ellia couldn't follow.

Timothy had said there were portals—*little rivers of power*—that tethered the realms together. Could they possibly be safe if they could somehow remain inside one of these rivers? Neither here nor there, so to speak. It was worth a try.

"Little rivers of magic," Erik said.

"What?"

"He described them as little rivers of magic. Maybe I'm being too literal, but I have an idea."

Erik didn't know exactly how Rachel had managed to transport them through the realms, but he remembered the first time he had done it, completely on accident when he had been running. His mind had to be empty of all thought. Like meditating.

He prepared himself to experience the tingling sensation that was about to erupt in every nerve ending simultaneously.

And then, as his mind cleared, so did the world around them.

Even before anything tangible emerged out of the white fog, the familiar and peaceful sound of flowing water eased into his mind.

Then the world re-formed, and Erik found himself standing next to Rachel, on a small sandbar in the middle of the Upper Iowa River. Not fifty feet away were the tents he and John slept in at that very moment.

But more importantly, just in front of them, was their canoe.

"Get in, quick," Erik said.

Rachel gave him a questioning look, but stepped in nevertheless.

Erik waded into the water, dragging the canoe into the current, and hopped in himself.

He shoved off against the rocky land just as a flash of light deposited Timothy and Ellia on the island where they had just been standing.

"Clever," Timothy said.

Ellia was already raising her hand and forming a ball of plasma in her palm. It shot out from her fingertips, but simply dissipated when it left the shore.

She tried it again, but it was as if an invisible wall of air was absorbing the energy of the plasma.

By now, they had paddled several hundred yards down river, and Timothy, Ellia, the sandbar, and the two tents pitched there were quickly receding into the darkness.

A bright, warm glow on the horizon betrayed the presence of a not-yet-risen moon. It would be a full moon, Erik knew. At least, it was the last time he'd been here. This was the very same night he and John had camped on the river. That seemed like an eternity ago now. Erik remembered that night very well, remembered being woken by a commotion in the middle of the night. But when he needed to relieve himself, and when he crawled out of his tent, still half-drunk, the night was quiet once again. He hadn't seen anyone else on the island, and the canoe had certainly still been there in the morning.

But now Rachel was seated at the front of that very canoe, facing him.

Erik managed a smile for her. "I think we're safe here," he said. But he wondered what type of grandfather-paradox stealing one's own canoe implied.

Watching the canoe recede towards the horizon, becoming merely a silhouette under the horizon-bound moon, already Timothy was conjuring his next move. Manipulating mortals and toying with time was a game that required its players to think three and four moves ahead. One move determined the next, which determined the next, which, sometimes, then affected a prior move. Cause and effect. Effect and cause. It was the sequencing that made all the difference.

"I'm beginning to think we are chasing ghosts," Ellia hissed. "They always seem to vanish right before our eyes."

Timothy turned to her with a scowl. Before he had time to reply, suddenly, a dancing point of light appeared in his vision. The light was blinding, hovering close to his face, looking like nothing more than a large firefly of pure light.

A voice came from the light. "I agree with your dark companion. This seems a latter Lammas."

Timothy scoffed. "Latter Lammas. What an arcane term. At least when the dark lady speaks, she insults me directly, instead of through innuendo." Timothy said, turning to Ellia. "For which she will suffer dearly."

"Time grows small, yet you continue to prance around in a wrinkled corporeal shell," the pulse rate of the point of light grew faster now, simpatico with its rising agitation. "Chasing your two pet mortals through this maze of time you have constructed."

"I'm well aware of the time shortage, Empress. Did I not just deliver on my promise to seal the realm of the Amethyst people?"

"Did you not also let your two pets escape into a river of time which you could not penetrate? They are mere mortals. And this is a wild goose chase."

"I am not chasing wild geese! I am hunting humans!"

That gave the firefly pause. Its pulse slowed for a few languid moments.

"The mortals are from Earth?" the voice asked then.

"Ah, so you do remember," Timothy cooed. "Without me, the universe would have been annihilated and our own people would have been homeless and starved to death ten thousand years ago. You will show me the respect I have earned, Empress," Timothy said. "Earth, as you no doubt remember, is a binary system that used to be an integrated reality. *I* divided the realms. *I* saved time. And it truly was an ingenious idea, using the indigenous civilizations' own temporal transportation technology to cause their dimensions to splinter."

"Please, save us your self-aggrandizing rants. We've had to listen to you for ten millennia, and never a moment's peace. How much longer do you plan to rest on your laurels?"

"I am not resting on my laurels!" Timothy pined. "You are acting like a human child, *Empress*, throwing a tantrum, *I want it now! now, now, now!* That reminds me of an earth-child's rhyme I'm rather fond of. Let's see if I can remember it. Ah, yes....

The space-time continuum sat on a wall.
The space-time continuum took a great fall.
Then along came Timothy, a little old man,
And put space-time back together again.

The pulsing light morphed into a deeper crimson, and Timothy knew it had took his meaning. "You plan on fusing the earth-time binary again?"

Timothy gave a conceited smile. "A stitch in time."

"How? And why do you fear these two mortals that you chase?"

"Is there no end to your incessant questions? I don't fear the mortals, Empress. They themselves will be the ones to put their reality back together again."

TIME WITHOUT END: BOOK II

World Without Time

C H A P T E R

1

E RIK HAD OFTEN WONDERED WHAT IDENTICAL twins saw when they looked at each other. Did they see more differences, or more similarities? Erik now realized the answer posed a bit of a paradox. Looking out over a sweeping vista of Earth's twin sister, it was the eeriness of the similarities that made the differences so noticeable.

Rachel was looking out over the panorama and pointing towards a small break in the pattern of rolling, tree-shrouded hills.

"Ji equis donor gefrois ji helas moktunkalli dumolar ti koe," Rachel said.

Erik stared at her blankly. Then Rachel spoke more of the

alien-sounding syllables. Their cadence, an iambic pentameter type of rhythm, had the same sound as English, but Erik couldn't understand a word.

"Is that your own language? I can't understand you."

This time it was Rachel's turn to cast Erik a blank look.

"And you probably have no idea what I'm saying, either," Erik said, more to himself than to her.

This made no sense. He and Rachel had been communicating clearly in all of the other realms they had passed through since the time they met. Why was this time different?

Erik tried using signs to get his meaning across. He pointed to his ear and shook his head, saying, "I can't understand you." Then shrugged his shoulders. "Why?"

Rachel spread her arms wide, as if to give a great big bear hug to the entire world around her. Then she pointed to herself. *"Koso molarkoni dumos."*

Erik took her meaning to be, because we're here, now, in my world.

But why would that make a difference? Erik thought. Then there was another thought accompanying that one.

But not a thought communicated in words, but rather a series of images, who's meaning was unmistakable. The images were of the sacred cave and the fire and the Priestess' gathering.

"I remember how it was at first, in the caves," the images communicated, as if it actually was Rachel's voice coming into his mind. The thought was more than the sum of the vision, but seemed to piggyback into Erik's mind on the flow of images.

That wasn't my thought, Erik realized. *Rachel, can you understand me when I'm not speaking?*

Yes. I can. It's as it was in the caves.

The images coming now were of a great stone wall, with words chiseled into it that Erik couldn't read. The thought those images conveyed was, "Language seems to stand in the way of the actual thought."

The wall crumbled, but the chiseled words remained. "If we don't use language, we can communicate through thought alone."

"How is that possible?" Erik thought.

"I don't know. Some say the Priestesses can do this, too. Communicate telepathically with each other," Rachel's thoughts replied in another series of rushing images.

"This is going to take some getting used to," Erik thought. "Tell me what you started to say before."

Rachel pointed again to the small gap in the forest at the base of a valley near the horizon, and images of thatched-roof homes, children and tilled fields came unbidden.

"Where would your city be?" Rachel asked.

Erik recognized the lay of the land quite well. They stood on a tall rise overlooking what would have been the far north side of Decorah. The rolling hills that were dark green under an unbroken shroud of evergreens in this world was known as Palos Heights in his, one of the newest in a never-ending chain of subdivisions continually popping up. On his world, rooftops and treetops would have shared the job of crowning the hills.

"Everywhere? All of this is your city? That's huge!"

Rachel found such a large city hard to imagine. She pictured as many people as she possibly could, and then doubled it and then doubled that.

Then new images came into her mind from Erik that dwarfed her idea of huge. She didn't have a word for as many people as he was showing her.

"Ten thousand," he said aloud.

"Thousand," she repeated, testing out the alien syllable on her tongue.

"It's actually a pretty small city by our standards," Erik thought. "Many of our cities have …. well, millions of people living in them. The largest city on my planet has about thirty million people and —this always struck me as ironic—it's on an island."

"Thirty million people on one island?"

Rachel pictured as many people as she possibly could, and imagined all of those people all getting onto one boat together. Then the boat sunk.

Erik laughed. And they both saw the image of the boat rising back up from the sea. "No, the island won't sink."

"What is it called?"

"The world's biggest city?"

"Yes."

"Tokyo," Erik said aloud.

The word sounded completely alien to Rachel.

"And what about your village?" Erik wondered. "Does it have a name?"

"Unfes," she said.

"Unfes," Erik rolled the alien word over his tongue.

"And how many people live in Unfes?"

Rachel considered that for a moment, and all the people standing on the boat vanished.

"You don't know. You've never counted," Erik understood. "Your people don't think in terms of quantity and empirical data like mine do, I'd guess."

Rachel continually surprised him. She seemed to understand concepts like evolution, technology, the Universe, a multiverse, a chronosverse—that's actually one Erik had a hard time with himself. Yet despite grasping the enormity of concepts like that, she had never thought about how many people lived in her small village. Erik found it a fascinating contradiction to say the least, and, as they walked towards her home, he found himself excited and a bit apprehensive about what other incredible and alien fascinations her people might hold.

That interesting mix of emotion—excitement and sheer terror—had been following him around all day. He remembered when it first really hit him this morning, just before Rachel had warped them here.

Last night, out of sheer exhaustion, they'd both fallen asleep in the canoe. When dawn had broken much too abruptly for his liking, it seemed to bring with it a feeling of timelessness. Traveling between worlds left a sense of disorientation in its wake, which seemed to have a compounding affect with each jump. Jet lag didn't begin to describe it. Erik woke feeling rested but stiff, and with no anchor in time whatsoever, as though the past simply didn't exist—as though he had just been born. He had no idea how long he'd been asleep or what day it was—but it struck him that today was the beginning of a completely new life among an entirely different people.

He realized he'd felt this way once before. It was as though his experiences in Madagascar had been a dry run, and now, this was his chance to get it right.

"We're not far now," Rachel thought. "Maybe a mile away. I didn't want to have us magically appear too close to the village."

In his mind, even as he saw the image of thatched roof homes growing exponentially larger, Erik was quickly learning to regard the images that came to mind only subconsciously. The less attention he paid to the actual images themselves, the more their inherent meaning stood out.

"I don't know how my people would react to us instantly materializing out of thin air. As it is, I'm not sure how they're going to react to you," Rachel communicated.

She was actually a bit concerned about it.

On the river, after they'd made the decision to return home to her people, she felt as if a huge weight had been lifted, leaving behind only a sense of peace. Whatever their fate, it gave her comfort knowing that it would be one of their own choosing. Bathed in that peaceful feeling, Rachel had fallen asleep under moonlit skies.

In the light of day, Rachel now feared that her sudden return with a stranger wasn't going to be an easy thing to explain.

Cresting the final hill, looking down its steep slope, Rachel's fears were momentarily quelled by the comforting sensation of seeing her home again, after what felt like she'd been away for an eternity.

Probably a mere three or four miles across, the valley below was a soft bed of grass where the hills laid down to rest before standing up again and rolling gracefully away on the other side of the village.

Erik's eyes fell upon Unfes for the first time, a series of squat silhouettes hunching on the grasslands.

The sounds of kids playing carried up towards them from the valley below.

"Welcome home," Erik and Rachel thought at the same time, so that it was impossible to tell from whom the thought originated.

They both smiled.

As they pushed on, the buzz of people grew louder, too many overlapping voices to make out any words. Soon Erik saw a group of at least a dozen small children running up the slope to meet them. Both boys and girls were wore similar garb—sleeveless white shirts, knit with a material that looked as soft and lightweight as cotton—and brown leather leggings that went about two-thirds of the way down towards their bare feet. Any skin that wasn't covered by clothes was caked in dried mud.

They were chattering excitedly and swarmed towards Rachel and Erik like bees. Most were probably just six or seven years old, some younger, and they chattered on in the language Erik couldn't understand. They crowded up to him, and began tugging at his clothes and touching their fingers and palms to his skin, quite excitedly, like they had never seen anyone like him before.

Rachel spoke to the children in her language. Almost immediately, as one, the children took two steps back.

"What did you say to them?" Erik wondered.

"Nothing. Let's keep going."

The kids trailed back a fair distance, shadowing them.

Just close enough to clearly identify the first of the outlying structures, there stood a row of five men, spear-throwers, holding their weapons at forty-five degree angles at their sides, buts in the ground, spearheads pointed in the direction of the man next to them in line, so all the spears together formed a blockade of "V" shapes. Their meaning was clear to Rachel.

At least they aren't pointed at us, Erik thought, not entirely certain how to interpret the intentions of the welcoming committee. It was clearly a show of force, indicating the village had trepidations about the prospect of a stranger in their midst.

An elderly woman broke through the line of warriors.

Erik watched as she and Rachel embraced and shared words he could not understand, which brought chuckles from the children.

Rachel pointed to Erik and he heard his name. The woman fixed on him with a heavy, piercing gaze.

"This is Temara, Priestess of the clan of the Unfesi," came Rachel's thoughts into Erik's mind.

Erik nodded to indicate deference to the older woman. A white, billowing robe made out of that same cotton-like material billowed around her thin figure. Like Rachel, she too, possessed a certain ageless quality. Her countenance and posture was strong and straight, though her face was clearly set with the lines of age.

"It is my pleasure to meet you finally in person," Erik said aloud. "The last time we spoke was through the fire in the cave.

Temara's eyes grew harder, more skeptical, when she had heard Erik's alien speech and saw the confusion the words caused for Rachel.

Erik thought, "Ask if she recognizes me from the fire."

"He wants to know if you recognize him," Rachel said.

Temara set Erik in a gaze that seemed to soften, ever so slightly, and replied to Rachel.

For Rachel, it was less the act of translation when Temara spoke. She needed to find the images to represent Temara's words which she could pass along to Erik.

"Temara asked, 'Where is the other one was who was with you, the time being? You are merely his servant.'

Rachel added to that, *Temara might take this as an offense, that the time being himself had not come to the village.*

Erik spoke aloud, "He did not travel with us. Rachel and I traveled here alone. He betrayed us and tried to cause us harm."

Then he gave Rachel the images she needed to understand. This was a strange way to communicate indeed.

We can't tell her that, Rachel thought, and explained, "If Temara believes we have fallen out of favor with the time being, she'll banish you, and maybe me, from the village thinking to protect her people from suffering the same fate. She holds the time being in the highest regard. We'll find it no easy task trying to convince the Priestess otherwise. For now, we must honor Temara's beliefs."

Rachel said to Temara, "The time being wanted to escort me back personally, but Erik is a very honorable man and wished to take the duty upon himself."

This seemed to ease the tension slightly.

Temara spoke again and Rachel passed the thought along to Erik, "You may rest with us tonight. Join us and we both may benefit and learn from the shared experience of each other's company."

Erik nodded his appreciation and Temara turned, leading them into the village.

The children, seeing that the Priestess had accepted the stranger, dared to form a throng around him again, touching and grabbing out of their intense curiosity.

Rachel took hold of Erik's arm and thought, "It may be harder than I thought to convince my people to let you stay. I believe we have to explain at least some of what has happened. If we can make them understand, that's the first step in hopefully accepting you among us."

Erik sighed deeply, "I don't want to make this harder on you or your people, Rachel. Maybe I shouldn't even be here."

"Nonsense. Temara is not ruled by fear. She will not be afraid of you simply because you're not one of us—although others might. Temara can have much trepidation and with good reason—to her, all the Unfesi are her children. So it won't be easy, but if you can earn her respect, everyone else will accept you, too. Temara owns the respect of the Unfesi. Don't worry, you're off to a good start—she already knows you keep good company. For some reason I've never quite understood, she's always seemed to respect me well beyond my years."

About the Author

In addition to being a writer, Tom is a serial entrepreneur, the founder of ttDesigns, a web design company, and Scenes of Time: Nature and Wildlife Photography.

He has also worked as a Journalist and served in the Peace Corpse in Africa, where he taught English as a Second Language.

Tom is the author of three books. His non fiction works are *A People's History of Capitalism* and *The Evolution of Thought*. *Time Without End* is his first novel.

Tom lives in Kansas City, MO.

About the Publisher

Green Effect Media is an Indie Publisher founded in Chicago in 2008, currently based in Kansas City, MO. It publishes works by independent authors.

A People's History of Capitalism
This left-wing view of Capitalism explores how the history of the past 500 years of Western Civilization has been driven by a singular obsession: the accumulation of ever-more wealth.

Reminiscent of Howard Zinn's A People History of the United States, this leftist economic perspective poses some powerful questions.

A People's History of Capitalism is the story of the world Capitalists have built for us, how things came to be this way and what, if anything, we can do about it.

The Evolution of Thought proceeds from one assumption: the world is not what we think it is.

This unique series of provocative essays exposes the fine line between truth and myth and challenges us to ask why we believe what we believe. And then asks, "What if we're wrong?"

Could our entire worldview be a lie?

Journey to the Middle of the Earth
Today we are witnessing a climactic conflagration in our centuries-old conflict with Mother Nature. As much as you and me, all life on Earth will be impacted by the pivotal environmental choices humanity makes over the crucial next decades.
(Photo essays).